Sheryl
Happy 4th
Hope you enjoy
your family characters.
[illegible signature]

The Treasure of

PRESTER JOHN

The Treasure of PRESTER JOHN

Howard C. Humphrey

Pentland Press, Inc.
www.ivyhousebooks.com

PUBLISHED BY PENTLAND PRESS, INC.
5122 Bur Oak Circle, Raleigh, North Carolina 27612
United States of America
919-782-0281
www.ivyhousebooks.com

ISBN 1-57197-370-2
Library of Congress Control Number: 2003104553

Printed in the United States of America

To our friends—Corso, Darkey, Dean, Lawley, Ridley, Padget, Posner, Schwartz, and Young—for providing an interesting group of characters.

And to my readers for making them come to life.

PROLOGUE

12th Century A.D.

During the middle part of the twelfth century, a letter was delivered to Manuel Comenus, known as Manuel I, emperor of Byzantium. It was hand-delivered by messenger and identified the sender as Prester John, the legendary Christian king and high priest of India. The letter read:

If indeed you wish to know wherein consists our great power, then believe without doubting that I, Prester John, who reigns supreme, exceed in riches, virtue, and power all creatures who dwell under heaven. Seventy two Kings pay tribute to me. I am a devout Christian and everywhere protect the Christians of our empire, nourishing them with alms. We have made a vow to visit the sepulcher of our Lord with a great army, as befits the glory of our Majesty, to wage war against and chastise the enemies of the cross of Christ, and to exalt his sacred name.

Our magnificence dominates the Three Indias, and extends to Farther India, where the body of St. Thomas the Apostle rests. It reaches through the desert toward the place of the rising sun, and continues through the valley of deserted Babylon, close by the tower of Babel. Seventy-two provinces obey us, a few of which are Christian provinces, and each has its own King. And all their Kings are our tributaries.

In our territories are found elephants, dromedaries, and camels, and almost every kind of beast that is under heaven. Honey flows in our land, and milk everywhere abounds. In one of our territories no poison can do harm and no noisy frog croaks, no scorpions are there, and no serpents creep in the grass. No venomous reptiles can exist there or use their deadly power.

In one of the heathen provinces flows a river called the Physon, which emerging from Paradise, winds and wanders through the entire Province; and in it are found emeralds, sapphires, carbuncles, topazes, chrysalides, onyxes, beryls, sardonyxes, and many other precious stones.

During each month we are served at our table by seven Kings, each in his turn, by sixty-two Dukes, and by three hundred and sixty-five Counts, aside from those who carry out various tasks on our account. In our hall there dine daily, on our right hand, twelve Archbishops, and on our left, twenty Bishops, and also the Patriarch of St. Thomas, the Protopapas of Samarkand, and the Archprotopapas of Susa, in which city the throne of our glory and our imperial palace are situated.

If you can count the stars of the sky and the sands of the sea, you will be able to judge thereby the vastness of our realm and our power.

The letter was widely circulated throughout Europe. It created excitement everywhere that a great Christian king would come from the East to drive the Saracens from the Holy Land. Pope Alexander III, some twelve years after the letter, tried to contact Prester John. He wanted his help in bringing Asia under the influence of the Church. Prester John's army never came to participate in any of the Crusades. The army that did arrive in the early thirteenth century was the great Mongolian horde led by Genghis

Khan. No less a historian than Marco Polo, during his stay at the court of Genghis's grandson, Kublai Khan, claimed to have found the site of Prester John's court. Polo surmised that Khan had used the Prester's vast treasure to finance his conquests of all the land from the Pacific Ocean to the Danube River.

Prester John: myth or mystery, hoax or history? Perhaps no one can say for sure. This story assumes the letter was true.

ONE

Cape Elizabeth, Maine

"Frank and Mary Fuhrwerk are dead!" the stranger said as Clark opened the front door.

"What?" Clark said in amazement.

"I'm sorry to be the bearer of bad news, but I knew you were friends with my colleagues, Frank and Mary. I'm Randall O'Brien, Professor of Medieval History at Bowdoin College."

"Come in, please, come in. Let me get my wife. Lyn, can you come to the living room? Bad news about Frank and Mary."

Lyn came into the room, wiping flour from her hands from the cake she was making for the Keene family get-together scheduled for Sunday.

"This is Professor O'Brien, from Bowdoin," Clark started to introduce the man to Lyn.

"Yes, it's Randy to my friends. And I know that both of you, Clark and Lyn, were close to the Fuhrwerks."

"What's happened to them?" Lyn asked.

"They were killed during a robbery at their dig site in Ethiopia last night."

Frank and Mary had been the Keenes' next-door neighbors for over twenty years. He was an archeologist and taught at the University of Southern Maine in Portland. Mary was an expert on world religions. They had moved into a condo near the water about eight months earlier. Soon after that they had gone to Ethiopia to work on a site that some experts thought might have been the court of Prester John, a legendary early Christian king.

"How do you know it was a robbery?" Clark asked.

"They had apparently found some artifacts dating from the twelfth century and were trying to tie them to Prester John. Those items were taken when they were killed. They were staying in a tent at the dig, and there was little security."

"That's not like Frank. If he had something he thought was valuable, he would have put it in a safer place."

"They did have a few items stored in the museum in Addis Ababa. Most likely the things taken were recent finds not yet moved to the museum," O'Brien continued. "I'm here not just to tell you about your friends. I also have a proposition for you and your search firm, Janus International. How much do you know about Prester John?"

"Very little," he replied.

"I know a good bit more," Lyn said. "I had some long discussions with Mary before they left. Prester John was supposedly a very wealthy Christian king back in the 1100s. He wrote to the Emperor in Byzantium that he was bringing a huge army to drive the Saracens out of the Holy Land. But he never came, and some scholars think it was all a hoax."

"Frank didn't think so. That's why they went to Ethiopia," the professor said.

"I thought that Prester John was in India?" Lyn went on.

"Many experts put him there. At the time he wrote to the Emperor, the world maps of the time showed three Indias . . . the eastern part of the African continent, the Arabian peninsula, and India as we know it. All three jutted into the Indian Ocean. And

Marco Polo was certain he found the ruins of the Presbyter's city south of what is now Beijing, in China."

"You said you are a professor of medieval history, What's your opinion? Did he really exist?" Clark wanted to hear his conviction.

"I believe he was real. Let me give you some more history. In 1221, as the Fifth Crusade was leaving Egypt, Jacques of Vitry, the Bishop of Acre, a French prelate wrote the Pope, 'A new and mighty protector of Christianity has arisen. He is King David of India, who has taken the field of battle against the unbelievers at the head of an army of unparalleled size.' Earlier, around 1145, a Syrian clergyman, Hugh, the Bishop of Tabala, when he returned from the Orient, said 'A certain John, a King and Priest, who lives in the extreme Orient, beyond Persia and Armenia, fought the Persians. They called him Presbyter John and he beat the Persians. He was a descendant of the Magi. A Nestorian.' Hugh was trying to make a case that while there was a Prester John, it was unlikely he would come to the Holy Land any time soon. Otherwise, Pope Urban II couldn't get the European rulers to send Crusaders."

"It all sounds a little preposterous to me," Clark said.

"I agree," Lyn added. "But Mary seemed convinced."

The professor went on. "I'd agree too, but there is just enough evidence to suggest it might be true. And, if it is, it would be the world's largest unfound treasure trove. That's what I would like for your associates at Janus to find—Prester John's treasure."

"It's their kind of challenge, I'll say that," Lyn asserted. "They like looking for long-lost things."

"I agree, Lyn," Clark chimed in. "An unfound and perhaps huge treasure is sure to excite our colleagues, Ridley Taylor and Milt Young."

"Yes," O'Brien agreed. "I'm aware of their finding the 500-year-old lab notes of Dr. Faust; and the treasure chest of one of the English lords that went on the Third Crusade."

"We'll put the proposal to them," Clark started the sales pitch. "They usually work on a percentage of anything they find plus expenses up front. Normally its 25 percent of the find; and, in a case like this, it might be as much as $100,000 for expenses."

"I have a backer in this who wishes to remain anonymous, but I'm sure these terms would be acceptable," O'Brien replied.

"We'll talk with Taylor and Young at our offices in Rome today. We have our semi-annual board meeting there next week and can let you know if it's a go after that."

"That's fine. Thank you for hearing me out. And, again I'm sorry about Frank and Mary. The Fuhrwerks were friends of mine, too."

'We'll be in touch," Clark said as he let him out the door. Returning to the living room, he asked Lyn, "What do you think?"

"I think there's something fishy about Professor O'Brien. And I don't like anonymous backers. But the story of Prester John and the possibility of a grand treasure are what Janus is all about, and I think we should go for it."

"Me, too, honey. Let's call Rid and Milt."

TWO

Rome

Ridley Taylor and Milt Young were in their offices at Janus International when the call came from the Keenes in Maine. Milt answered and yelled to Rid, "Get on the phone. It's Clark and Lyn."

"Hey! It's good to hear from you," Rid said as he put the phone to his ear.

"It's good to hear you two also. How's business?" Lyn asked.

"Nothing big, but it's been steady with security audits for a number of American companies that have operations in Europe and the Middle East. All these potential terrorist threats make for good business," Rid replied.

"And we did locate one missing person, who wanted to remain lost. We turned that one over to a marriage counselor," Milt added.

"We may have our next big case," Clark started. He told them about the visit from Professor O'Brien and the deaths of the Fuhrwerks. "This Prester John must have amassed a great fortune that seems to have disappeared. Lyn has been doing some research on him. Tell them what you found, honey."

"Prester John was either very rich, living in Africa or Asia, or he was an invention of some Middle Ages monk who wanted to slow down the Fifth Crusade. In the twelfth century, a letter was hand-delivered to the Emperor of Byzantium. It was signed Prester John and it describe his kingdom, riches, and his plan to come west to drive the infidels from the Holy Land. It caused a number of European kings to delay signing on for the Crusade as they thought they should wait for this mysterious King and his army. There are a lot of discrepancies in research papers about this Presbyter. There really *was* a letter. Beyond that, there are as many locations for his court as there are research papers. Our friends the Furhwerks were looking for him in Ethiopia. Many believe that he followed the path of the Apostle Doubting Thomas, to India. Marco Polo spent time at Kublai Khan's palace in Peiping, China. He claimed to have found the Prester's Palace south of the Imperial City."

"Sounds like a tough assignment, but one right up our alley," Milt replied, with excitement.

"Tell us more about this Professor that wants to hire us," Rid requested.

"He is a Professor of Medieval History at Bowdoin College here in Maine. He claims he was helping the Fuhrwerks with their quest. He says he represents an anonymous backer who seeks the treasure. We told him, in that case, we would need up-front expense money of as much as $100,000, and 25 percent of any treasure found. He didn't flinch. He said his benefactor had the means to fund the search."

"Any idea who this anonymous Mr. Money Bags might be?" Milt asked.

'No," Lyn replied.

"I say let's ask for the 100 grand up front. If he comes up with that, we'll know his backer is serious," Rid offered.

"And 25 percent sounds real good. That's 5 percent more than we got for Lady JoAnna's ancestor's treasure in the New Millennium case," Milt added.

"You're all coming to Rome next week for our semi-annual board meeting," Rid continued. "Why don't we continue some research and we'll decide at the meeting if we want the case?"

"I'll call the other directors and fill them in so they can study this John guy, too," Milt said.

The directors of Janus included the Keenes, and Lady Jo and Lord Reggie Byerly from England. The Keenes were involved with Janus's first case, in which they found the 450-year-old notes of Dr. Faust about how to make gold. The Byerlies brought the next big case to Janus, involving a treasure chest lost by JoAnna's ancestor. Sir James Ompree, during the Third Crusade in the twelfth century. The other director, Countess Liesel Von Anton from Corfu, is the one whose ancestor hired Faust to make gold for him. Finally, though not a director by his choice, their main advisor is Monsignor Ricardo Corso, who is the curator of the Vatican Museum.

"Ricardo should be able to get any Vatican records about this Prester John," Rid said. "I'll go see him today while Milt calls the others."

"And I'll continue my research. We'll tell Professor O'Brien that a decision will be made next week at our meeting," Lyn stated.

"And I'll tell him that because his backer is to remain anonymous, we'll need the $100,000 up front," Clark said.

"All right," Rid opened. "You're scheduled to arrive at two PM on Tuesday. Right?"

"That's right," Lyn said. "And you've booked us in our favorite hotel, the Senato?"

"Yes, Georgio said he would have your favorite room ready," Ridley finished.

"We're planning dinner Tuesday night for all the board members at Dal Bolognese," Milt said. "Ricardo will also be there. We can discuss the case over dinner and then make our decision the next morning at our meeting. It's scheduled for 10 AM Wednesday in our office."

"All right. We'll see you at Dal Bolognese," Clark closed.

“There will be a limo just outside Customs to take you to the hotel,” Rid reminded them.

“Thanks. Clark and I are excited about the possibilities of finding what is perhaps the world’s richest treasure,” Lyn said as she thought of Prester John and Professor O’Brien’s anonymous benefactor. Then she thought to herself, “I wonder who his sponsor can be?”

THREE

Rome

The Keenes took a taxi to the restaurant, Dal Bolognese, arriving just before 8 PM. Reggie and JoAnna Byerly were already there, having martinis at the small bar. The maitre d' pointed them out when they asked for the table of Taylor or Young.

"Hi. My name is Clark Keene, and this is my better half, Lyn."

"We're the Byerlies. Reggie and Jo," he said.

"You're the two from Ridley's first case. The Faust affair," JoAnna added.

"Yes. And you are the ones who hired Janus to find your ancestor's treasure lost during the Third Crusade," Clark said.

"Right. We helped foil the plot of a very evil man, Sir Dean Floyd, who was trying to take over the world by privatizing the world's military," Jo replied,

"In our case we helped end the Gulf War by finding a 450-year-old list and notes from the original Dr. Faust," Lyn stated.

"This new case is like those other two in that it involves an ancient lost treasure. That of Prester John," Reggie proposed.

"Right. This Prester John is quite mysterious, isn't he?" Lyn replied.

"I never had heard of him until this Professor O'Brien appeared at our door," Clark added.

"I had heard a little about him from friends of ours," Jo said, "But with the reading I've done over the last few days, I'm not sure if he was real or just some hoax by a medieval monk."

"Hello Keenes and Byerlys," Milt Young interrupted the conversation. "I think you all know our advisor, Monsignor Corso, from the Vatican Museum."

"Yes. It's good to see you again, Ricardo!" Lyn said. "We look forward to our visits with you."

"Hello Father," Lady Jo said. "This is the first time my husband has been with me. Father Corso, this is Lord Reginald Byerly. Reggie, meet one of wisest men on earth, Monsignor Ricardo Corso, curator of the Vatican Museum."

"A real pleasure, sir," Reggie said as they shook hands.

"And for me. But please call me Ricardo. The 'sir' should be used for your title," he said as he kissed each of the ladies' hands.

"I go by Reggie."

"Here comes Ridley with Countess Von Anton," Milt pointed to them entering the restaurant. "Let's move to our private room."

Rid handled the introduction of Reggie and JoAnna to the elderly Countess.

"I have heard a great deal about you," Liesel Von Anton began. "How you hired these two to find your ancestor's chest. How you helped foil the scheme of Dean Floyd. And how you have converted your castle at Bodmin Moor into a fine school for young women."

"Yes. We have our first class now enrolled, and classes start in two weeks," Jo said proudly.

"That's good," said Rid. "Now let's get down to current business. Here's the waiter. I have preordered the pasta course: penne with their signature Bolognese sauce. So, please order whatever main course you like. I recommend the Cotolleta Milanese or their special Bolito Misto. But everything is good."

After the waiter brought both red and white wines from Emilia-Romama and left the room, Ridley went on. "First I want the Keenes to retell the story of the approach by this Professor O'Brien."

Clark and Lyn each interrupted the other as they together told of the Professor's news about the deaths of the Fuhrwerks, and how he wanted to hire Janus to find the lost treasure of Prester John. They then mentioned the anonymous benefactor who was funding the search.

"Whoever it is, he must be for real," Clark said as he pulled a cashier's check from his inside coat pocket. "I told O'Brien last Friday that we would be meeting today and tomorrow to decide if we want the case. I also told him that since his backer was anonymous, we wanted $100,000 expense money up front, He delivered this check for the full amount on Monday."

"All right," Milt said. "It's apparent Mr. Anonymous is serious."

"He must believe Prester John was real," Liesel added.

"I believe he was real," the Monsignor began. "We have extensive records on him in our Vatican Library. He lived in the twelfth century somewhere in what he called India. Unfortunately, at that time there were three Indias . . . Ethiopia, Arabia, and the current India. Some scholars even placed him in China."

"Our friends were digging in Ethiopia when they were killed," Lyn said.

"There is support for the site of his court being there. There is also support for his having been in China. You all know Marco Polo placed him just south of present-day Beijing," the Curator continued. "Perhaps the most telling evidence is from the Presbyter's own hand. Here are copies of the original letter delivered to the Byzantine Emperor, Manuel I. Near the end of the letter, he mentions Samarkand and the city of Susa. There was such a city. It was in the steppes of what is now the Uzbekistan."

"Do you think he may have moved his court and treasure around his seventy-two kingdoms?" Rid queried.

"He may have. He also mentions a desert with both camels and dromedaries. They come from different places. So there is no conclusive location. We're still studying other references," Corso concluded.

Lyn began, "A French Bishop named Vitry went in search of the Prester. He called him King David who, we know, lived centuries earlier. In any event he said this King David was himself commonly called Prester John. He reported that the Caliph of Baghdad had written P.J. That's what I've been calling him. The Caliph was being threatened by a rival, the Shah of Kwarezm. Vitry's reports of King David's victories and steady advance toward the Holy Land were joyfully received throughout Europe. Prester John was finally coming to free Jerusalem."

"I'll see what we have on this Bishop Vitry," Corso said.

"The book I am quoting from, I brought with me," Lyn resumed. "It's called *The Realm of Prester John.* It's by Robert Silverberg and published by Doubleday in 1972. He explores all of the myths and mysteries surrounding P.J. Anyway, Silverberg concluded that Vitry was correct in his descriptions of the advancing army, but wrong as to who it was. This warrior king was no Christian. Neither was he Prester John. He was Genghis Khan. He wasn't coming to free the Holy Land either. His plan was to conquer Islam and, after that, all of Christendom. In fact, his aim was to conquer the whole world."

Reggie broke in, "I'd say we need some more study on Genghis Khan, too!"

"Definitely," Milt replied. "I'm making notes, and we'll each have an assignment before we leave tonight."

The waiter and his assistant returned with the pasta course Rid had ordered for all. "Our famous Bolognese meat sauce over penne," the waiter proudly announced, When he had left, Rid continued, "Liesel, have you found anything about this P.J., as Lyn has renamed him?"

"Not as much as the others," the Countess replied. "My friends who live with me were excited to have the assignment. The best the four of could do was a reference in Shakespeare. I wrote down the quote. It's from the second act of *Much Ado about Nothing.* The character Benedik is pleading with the King to give him an assignment so he could prove his loyalty. He says, 'Will your Grace command me any service to the world's end. I will go on the slightest errand now to the Antipodes that you can devise to send me on; I will fetch you a toothpick now from the furthest inch of Asia; bring you the length of Prester John's foot; fetch you a hair from the Chan's beard; do you any embassage to the Pigaries . . . you have no employment for me.' Good prose, but I'm not sure it's helpful," she concluded.

"From that, it appears Shakespeare thought P.J. was a trivial thing. But in the same quote, he references the great Chan, which could be a reference to Genghis Khan," Milt interpreted.

"Could be," added Rid. He paused while the main courses were served. When they were alone again, he continued, "We have Genghis Khan, the three Indias, Susa, Samarkand, Ethiopia. A lot of places to start. Anybody have any thing else to add."

"I forgot to tell you that Silverberg said that Marco Polo was convinced that Genghis Khan killed the Prester. He also thought it might have been an earlier Khan, Togrul, who was the Khan of the Christian Kerait's Mongols."'

"Let's do this," Rid said, "Ricardo, you and the Keenes continue the study of Prester John himself, including anything more to pinpoint the site of his court. Milt, you and the Byerlys start a review on Genghis Khan, looking for any reference to P.J. Countess, you can rest in the morning. We'll set back the board meeting until 3 PM to see what else we find."

"Still at Janus headquarters?" Clark asked.

"Yes," said Rid, "You can study till then. Let's find this mysterious Prester John."

As the main course and more wine was served, dinner conversation turned to small talk. But as everyone left for their hotels or apartments, all had the same thought: "Prester John, who and where are you?"

FOUR

Rome

At 3 PM the next day, all of Janus International's board of directors were in their seats around the conference room table. Their advisor, Monsignor Corso, was also there. Milt Young called them to order, saying, "Let's see if our morning studies have yielded any more clues about Prester John. Will you and the Keenes start us off, Ricardo?"

"We spent the morning focusing on two things: The letter from Prester John and the writings of Bishop Vitry. I took apart the letter, and Lyn and Clark read everything the Vatican Library had on Vitry. I'll tell you what I found and then they will tell you their findings. The first clue in the letter is where P.J. says he has seventy-two kings under his rule. In the twelfth century, there was no place on earth that had seventy-two kingdoms. He probably was referencing tribes. There were hundreds of those in Asia at that time. This supports the site being in China. The next clue is his reference to the grave of St. Thomas the Apostle as being in Farther India, which again could be China. About 200 years ago, some Portuguese missionaries claimed to have found the tomb of the saint known as

Doubting Thomas and they took the body to Ethiopia. That supports both China and Ethiopia. He mentions a desert that reaches to the place of the rising sun. That could be the high desert around Beijing. It also could be the Gobi, the Sahara, or the Negev Desert. Not very conclusive. The other end of his kingdom, he describes as the valley of deserted Babylon, close by the tower of Babel. This would put him in the Middle East, south of what he describes as Samarkand. So, what's my best guess? China, near Beijing. Probably the site Marco Polo claims to have found."

"Thank you, Ricardo. How about your morning, Lyn?" Rid said.

"Not a whole lot more on Bishop Vitry. He wrote a chronology of Prester John. Some of the dates don't seem to match. P.J.'s letter was supposedly delivered around 1165. Genghis Khan did his conquering about fifty years later."

"He captured Beijing in 1215. We have his life story," interrupted JoAnna. "By 1215, this Prester would most likely be in his seventies."

"Good," continued Lyn. "Vitry, and others, thought the Prester may have been a reincarnation of the Apostle John, who could have written as many as five books of the New Testament. The Apostle did refer to himself as a Presbyter. But these two are more than 1,200 years apart. And Silverberg, in his research, disputes Vitry's claim that P.J. was killed by Genghis Khan. More important, though, Silverberg did believe that P.J. was killed by a khan, Those two claims tell Clark and me that China was, very possibly, the site of the Prester's Court."

"Sounds credible," Rid said. "Okay, Reggie, JoAnna, and Milt, let's hear about Genghis Khan."

"JoAnna, why don't you start? Then Reggie and I can fill in any blanks," Milt proposed.

"All right. I've written out a timeline about Genghis Khan. I have made copies for each of you. You can read along with me." The copies read:

1162	Temüjin born. Taken as a slave by a rival tribe. Escapes as a young man.
1190	Temüjin wages war with rival tribes.
1204	Defeats Naimans and Merkts tribes.
1206	Temüjin is chosen Khan of all the Mongols. Takes the name Genghis Khan, meaning "king of kings."
1207	First war against Korea.
1215	Capture of Peking.
1217	The Khan returns to Karakorum.
1219	Mongols attack Khwarezm.
1220	Capture of Bokhara and Samarkand.
1224	Khan's aides Tebe and Subatai go to Russia.
1225	Khan returns to Mongolia.
1227	Khan dies.
1229	Ögödai elected Khan.
1237	Aides Batu and Subatai invade Europe.
1241	Death of Ögödai. Mongols withdraw from Europe.
1246	Till 1260, Kuyuk and Mango are Khans.
1260	Genghis's grandson, Kublai Khan, reigns until 1294. Moves Court to Forbidden City.
1275	Marco Polo at Kublai's court till 1292.

"The research book I took this from is Harold Lamb's *Genghis Khan and the Mongolian Horde*, published by Random House in 1954."

Milt said, "I took that same book home last night. It tells a fascinating story of the Mongols' war tactics. They were fierce in battle. Excellent horsemen. After taking a city they massacred most of the townspeople. The others they would run as interference, in front of the army at the next town. When larger cities were taken, they killed only the leaders and put one of the Khan's generals in as Governor. Lamb concluded that next to Alexander the Great, Genghis Khan made more change in the world in one lifetime than anyone else in history, His realm ran from the Pacific Ocean to the Danube River."

Reggie chimed in, "I read the encyclopedia about the Khan. The Mongols were not religious. Like the American Indians and other nomadic peoples, they worshiped the sky. Warmth, rain, the seasons all came from the sky as did stars at night and eclipses. The Khan was the law. His basic rules were called Yasak. He had three that were the base of all others. They were: No Mongol should be a slave. Mongols are above all other men. They must obey the Khan.

"The Khan could neither read nor write. He entrusted administration of his empire to the Uighurs, the only Mongols who could write. After the capture of Peking, he found a member of China's Royal Court, Lu Chu Tsai, who was very intelligent. Khan took him for his personal scribe and he became the King's most trusted advisor. He developed new laws for the Yasak. One said 'All men should believe in one God.' Khan added, 'That each man could make their own choice of who to worship by their own custom.' Khan's army was organized into Gurans of 1,000 men. Each man had five horses. They would ride one each day and then give it four days' rest. Another of the Khan's laws said 'Steal a horse = Death.' or 'Leave a warrior group of 10 = Death.' Perhaps, most important for today, I found that Karakorum was his capital city in Mongolia, and what was called Khwarezm is now Iran."

"That's all good work. Thank you all. Now to the big question. Do we take the case?" Rid questioned the group.

Each in turn voted yes.

Rid went on, "I agree. Jo and Reggie, I know you have classes beginning soon, but if you have an extra day or so, I'd like for you to go with Milt to Venice to see if they have Marco Polo's journals. I will go with Clark and Lyn to Ethiopia to see what their friends may have found. Countess, if you like, you can join either group."

"I'll go to Venice. I always like it there," Liesel answered.

"And I would like to go with you and the Keenes to Ethiopia, Rid," Corso said.

"Okay. Clark, will you contact Professor O'Brien and tell him we're on the case? You can review with him what we've found thus far, and what our next steps will be," Milt proposed.

"I'll call him when we adjourn," Clark replied.

"That's sooner than you think," Rid said. "We were going to use this meeting as a brainstorming session about where to find new clients. This case will use all our time for a while, so we'll hold off on the prospecting and put it on our next meeting agenda. By the way, that meeting is currently scheduled for October 10. Is that all right with everyone?" All nodded their approval.

"Here are copies of our financial statements. We're still flush from our share of JoAnna's ancestor's treasure. Take them with you. If you have any questions, give us a call," Rid said as he passed out the statements.

"Then let's adjourn to the bar at the Hassler. I've made dinner reservations there for tonight," Milt said. "Meeting adjourned."

Each left the meeting with a feeling of excitement over finding the treasure of Prester John. Each also had a sense of danger about what might lie ahead.

FIVE

Mongolia

"Subotai," the Khan ordered. "Go get Borcho and Chepe, Bring them to my yurt."

"I obey my great Khan, Temüjin," Subotai replied as he bowed and backed away.

Temüjin was his name. He was born the son of the Khan of the Kiyat Mongol Tribe, Yesugai. His mother was a captive from another tribe. During his youth he constantly practiced his horsemanship and wrestling. These were the Mongols' favorite sports. He was betrothed to the daughter of the Khan of a neighboring tribe at the age of nine. He lived with that tribe for four years. They frequently traded with the Chinese caravans. Temüjin saw silks and riches beyond his imagination.

His father died when Temüjin was thirteen. He returned to his tribe to claim his birthright, but the Kiyats deserted the boy Khan. He was captured by the Taijuts who put him in a yoke they called a kang. With help from a tribesman, he escaped. He swore vengeance. He recruited his warriors and when strong enough, he claimed his bride. Over the next few years he conquered most of the other tribes of the nomadic Mongols, who were always fighting over the best hunting grounds. Finally, Temüjin controlled all of the high plains between China and Siberia. He changed his name to Genghis Khan. They called him the Khan of Khans, or king of kings. It was time for him to take his army and go after the riches of the world he had seen as a youth.

His three leading warriors entered the Khan's yurt, bowed, and sat at his command.

"Borchu, Subotai, and Chepe, you are my most trusted generals. I call you together to say to you it is time for us to reach beyond this high desert. We must exercise our strength and make war on China."

The three nodded their approval. "We have little experience at warfare on foreign soil," Subotai said.

"True, Subotai. It is my plan to first conquer Korea. They are small and weak. It will train our warriors for bigger things," the Khan replied.

"What about China's Great Wall?" Chepe asked.

"I have a plan for that. We will hold daily tournaments of wrestling and riding just outside the wall. The guards will become accustomed to us being there without trying to get through the wall. When they become complacent, we win storm the wall and open gates for our horsemen."

"It should work, my great Khan," Borchu agreed.

"Yes," added Chepe and Subotai.

"Begin longer training rides today. Each warrior is to have five horses. He'll ride one and rest the others in turn for four days. Speed will be one of our most important weapons. The other, even more important, is fear. We must be ruthless. When we take a village, burn it to the ground and kill all the villagers. Take all their valuables as plunder and distribute it to the troops. I will still get my tithe from each of them at tax time. It's time for the Mongols to be recognized. We leave for Korea in one week."

Korea was taken in less than a month, There was much nervousness in the Chinese Emperor's court that this horde of unrefined fighters might next turn on them. The Emperor's chief of staff, Ye Liu Kutsai, tried to calm them by saying the wall would hold them out. "We will double the guards on the wall, Emperor. They will not get through."

But the Khan's ploy worked. After six weeks of daily games outside the wall, the Chinese lost interest and became complacent. The Mongolian horde broke through the wall and world history was forever changed. After the surrender of China to Genghis Khan, he knew his army could conquer the world. That became his ambition. He took Ye Liu Kutsai as his personal slave and scribe. There were stories of a Christian king with a great treasure hiding in a valley south of Peiping. Khan sent out search parties. They found an empty palace of this so-called King, Prester John. But the King wasn't there. They marveled at the mosaic floor in the main hall. It was a map of all the known world. There were seventy-two fish scattered across the map. When they brought the Khan to see the map, he smiled and said, "Someday this will all be mine. Kutsai, have a copy made of this map. It will help guide us in our conquest."

Ye Liu told the Khan that he heard this Presbyter had gone west and was somewhere in the steppes. He told the Khan that the fish was an early Christian symbol and the places on the map may be other locations belonging to this Prester John.

"Till now, Kutsai. Now they belong to Genghis Khan."

The Khan could neither read nor write, but he wanted a record of their conquests. The two men became very close and Ye Liu became Khan's most trusted advisor. Ye Liu helped write the Mongol laws, the Yasak. As their army was moving across Asia, he once told the Khan, "You can conquer others from the saddle, but you can't govern them from there."

Genghis Khan revised his tactics and began leaving his officers in each captured city to govern and collect taxes. He still would take the stronger ones and run them as interference in front of his army as fodder at the next city. When they would come to one of the cities marked with a fish, they would find a place of Christian worship. Each had a cross, a statue of Prester John, and a small treasure. They took them all.

One day a pilgrim from a passing camel caravan came to the Khan in his yurt with a message from the Caliph of Baghdad.

"What is the message?" the Khan ordered of the messenger.

"I do not know, Great Khan of Khans. It is tattooed on the top of my head, now covered by my hair," the pilgrim stammered.

"Shave his head," Genghis Khan bellowed.

The message revealed was a request for the Khan's help in fighting Muhammed Shah of nearby Persia. The Khan decided that both the Caliph and Shah would pay for his guarantee of peace between them. He sent two envoys to the Shah with his proposal. The envoys were killed, so Genghis Khan moved further west and conquered them both.

Parts of his army went north to control Russia and the steppes of the Ukraine. Finally, after crossing the steppes in winter, the Khan set up his headquarters in Samarkand.

"This is the place to where Prester John supposedly came. Perhaps his vast treasure is here," Ye Liu said to the Khan.

"Then search for it. I am growing weary of war. I plan to leave my son Ögödai in charge here. I will return to my desert at Karakorum to live out my days. If the treasure is found, send half of it to me."

Genghis Khan did return to the place of his birth and died in 1227. He had named his son, Ögödai, to succeed him. The army's move west halted at the Danube River as most of the warriors were ready to go home. The Mongols had achieved an Empire to rival that of Rome; but, like Alexander the Great, they did it in one lifetime. Genghis's favorite grandson, Kublai, succeeded Ögödai. He moved his capital to Peiping and built the Imperial City. During his reign Marco Polo was a guest at his court.

Whether Genghis Khan ever found the treasure of Prester John remains, like everything else about this ancient Christian King, a mystery. The legend of the treasure enticed fortune hunters through the centuries to the present day.

SIX

Venice

The morning after the board meeting, Milt Young, Countess Liesel von Anton, along with JoAnna and Reggie Byerly took the 9:30 Alitalia flight from Rome to Venice, arriving at 11:05. The Countess checked into her favorite hotel, the Danieli, and the others went to the more modest Savoia & Jolanda, two doors farther along the Riva della Schivione from St. Mark's Square. Milt had called ahead and arranged a 4 PM appointment with the Librarian of the San Georgio Church. Marco Polo had been a member of that church, and the guide books had said it housed Polo's writings about his travels to the Far East. San Georgio was across the Grand Canal from the hotels. Milt knew the Number 1 Vaporetto went directly from Schivione to San Georgio before working its way up the Grand Canal. At 3:50 PM they got off the water bus and went to the side door of the basilica.

The door opened and a rather rotund priest said, "Welcome travelers. I am Father Cesar Saputo. Chief Librarian of San Georgio is one of many titles and duties I carry. We don't get many calls about Marco Polo. Just researchers working on that period of history. But you called yesterday, and I have had another call this morning. That wasn't part of your group, was it?"

"No," replied Milt. "Our group is all here. I am Milt Young. I called yesterday. This is Countess von Anton from Corfu, and these are Lord and Lady Byerly from England."

"A pleasure to have such distinguished guests," the Priest said. "Please, follow me to the Library."

Along the way, the team was speculating on who the other caller might have been.

"Clark called Professor O'Brien yesterday after our meeting. I wonder if he called," Reggie said.

"Yes, Clark told him we were coming here," JoAnna added.

"He's hired us to locate the treasure," Milt queried. "So why would he follow us?"

"Maybe he's in a hurry," Reggie stated.

"Or his anonymous benefactor is," observed the Countess.

"I sure would like to know who called," Jo said.

"Me, too," Milt agreed as they arrived at the Library.

It was not a large room and looked more like a den than a Library. One wall was bookshelves from floor to ceiling, two were covered with filing cabinets, and the fourth was large windows looking toward the Lido.

"Our Marco Polo collection is in these two cabinets. But you can't have the originals. The paper is too brittle to be handled. The notes were translated into German and English in the sixteenth century, and we have transferred those notes to microfilm. I assume you want the English version," Saputo said as he handed a folder to Milt.

"Thank you. Where should we work?" Milt replied.

"Here. We have a microfilm reader and you can make a paper copy from that if you like. May I help you find something?" the Priest asked.

'We're interested in all his travels, but particularly in the period when he stayed at the Court of Kublai Khan," Milt responded.

"That would be the last few years of the thirteenth century. Those notes are all in this folder and on one set of microfilm."

Milt said, "Cesar, do you have a second viewer? It would cut our time in half."

"I have one in my office. I'll get it."

"Thank you. All right, let's get to work. Jo, you and Liesel take this card of film. It's labeled for the years 1275 to 1285. Reggie and I will take his later years at Peiping, 1286 to 1292. Make a copy of anything that refers to Prester John, or treasure, or conquest, or Genghis Khan. If you're not sure, copy it. Okay?"

"Yes," replied Jo and Liesel together.

The priest returned with the second reader and then left them alone to their work. The group read for about three hours through the chronology of the travels of Marco Polo. They were amazed at the accuracy of his descriptions of places that were still identifiable today. At 7 PM, Father Saputo came in to the room and said he was closing for the night.

"May we take the film and readers to our hotel for overnight?" Milt asked the priest.

"No, I'm sorry. We only have the one set of microfilm and so we don't let it out," Cesar said.

"I understand. What time tomorrow is your other caller coming?" Milt innocently inquired.

"At 2 PM.

"May we come in the morning? We should be done before two."

"The library opens at 10, but I am here by 8:30. I could let you in then."

"We'll be here," Milt answered. "Thank you again, Father, for all your help. We can find our way out."

After leaving the church, the group took another Vaporetto ride three stops up the canal to the stop by the Academia Museum. Just a short walk down a narrow passageway brought them to Milt's favorite restaurant, the Taverna San Trovaso. The place was busy with a line out the door waiting to be seated. Milt had made a reservation and had been there many times. When the owner saw him in line he waved them forward, saying, "Your reserved table is waiting, Mr. Young. It's nice to see you again. Where is your American friend?"

"In Ethiopia. I had first choice, so I took Venice," Milt said with a smile.

"A wise choice. Here is your table," the owner said as he pointed to the prime table in the front alcove of the main dining room.

The pasta, fish, meat, house wines, and desserts were all excellent. About 10 PM, the group left the restaurant and returned to their hotels via the Vaporetto. Both the dinner and boat conversation centered on who else was looking into Prester John.

"We will know tomorrow," Milt told them. "I plan to be outside when the other party shows up."

"It's so mysterious," the Countess said.

"Yes, Liesel, and exciting as well. Perhaps our looking has caused interest by someone other than the Professor and his benefactor."

"It's too coincidental to be anyone other than the Professor," Reggie argued.

"Not if someone monitored calls to the San Georgio Library. It could be anybody. We're talking about a huge treasure. Perhaps the largest the world has ever known," Milt said as they reached their hotels.

They saw the Countess to the door of the Danieli. She said, "Good night. I won't go with you in the morning. I need to rest. JoAnna reads much faster than I do anyway."

"That's fine. We'll let you know what we find," Milt agreed.

"What a lovely lady," Jo said as they walked on to their hotel.

"She was part of your Faust affair, wasn't she?" Reggie remembered.

"Yes, it was her ancestor, the original Count von Anton, that hired Faust to make gold. We tested his formula and it was worthless," Milt explained.

"Let's hope this turns out better," Jo interjected. "I'm very concerned about this other party. I have this strange feeling of danger."

"I'll carry my Walther tomorrow, just in case," Milt tried to soothe her.

They retrieved their room keys at the desk and said good night. Each went to bed with that same feeling of foreboding that JoAnna had expressed.

SEVEN

Ethiopia

While Milt and his team were in Venice, Ridley Taylor, Monsignor Corso, and Clark and Lyn Keene had arrived in Addis Ababa, Ethiopia. They made arrangements through their hotel concierge for a van with an English-speaking driver for the next morning. They wanted to go out to the dig site of the Fuhrwerks. The desk clerk told them the Fuhrwerks had stayed in the same hotel, but the police had taken all their belongings.

"Who is in charge of the investigation?" Rid asked.

"Captain Hakeem Olajoni. A very capable man," the clerk replied. "You can reach him at the main police station."

"Thank you," Rid replied. "You three put your things away in your rooms. Then come to mine and we'll plan our day for tomorrow. It's after 5 PM now, so I'll have cocktails sent up and make a dinner reservation in the hotel dining room. Be at my room, 321, by 6:30."

After the others left the lobby, Rid asked the concierge/desk clerk to reserve a table for either four or five people at 8 PM that evening.

"You're expecting a guest?" the clerk asked.

"I plan to invite the police detective," Rid replied.

Rid went to his room to call Captain Olajoni. His first efforts with the supposedly direct-dial phone were futile. Finally he dialed the hotel operator and asked him to put the call through. Moments later, the police Captain was on the line.

"Captain Olajoni, my name is Ridley Taylor. I am here with friends of the victims, Frank and Mary Fuhrwerk, in your current investigation."

"I've been wondering when someone would show up inquiring about them," he replied in perfect English.

"Your English is very good," Rid complimented him.

"I studied at Cambridge. And call me Hakeem, please. We are not so formal here."

"Okay, Hakeem. I go by Rid. I've made a dinner reservation here at the Hotel Movenpick for our group at eight. I'd like to have you join us to bring us up to date on the investigation."

"You're buying? Police work doesn't pay much here."

"Of course. Then we'll see you at eight?"

"I'll be there."

Rid then unpacked his carry-on bag. He felt a little naked because he didn't bring a gun.

As if rehearsed, the room service cart, the Keenes, and Father Corso all arrived together at 6:30. Rid told them of his invitation to the policeman.

"We should make a list of the questions we have for him," Lyn suggested.

"A good idea," Ricardo added. "For sure we want to know all there is about the Fuhrwerks' deaths.

"Yes," said Clark. "And what was stolen from the camp that night."

"In fact," the Monsignor continued, "I'll want to know what artifacts have been taken to the National Museum and why they think they might be related to Prester John."

"That would be a good activity for you tomorrow, while the three of us go out to the dig," Rid agreed.

"What about a visit to the National Library to see if they have anything on Prester John?" Lyn offered.

"Another good idea. Why don't you follow that trail, Lyn? Clark and I can go to the dig. You up to a ride in the desert, Clark?"

"Sure."

The group had their cocktails and proceeded to dinner at eight. Captain Olajoni was waiting in the lobby.

"You must be Hakeem," Rid said as he shook the small, thin man's hand.

"At your service, Mr. Taylor. And you must be the Keenes from America. And we are honored Monsignor Corso to have such a distinguished visitor in our small country."

"I'm excited to be here. We believe the Fuhrwerks were on the verge of a major discovery related to our faith," Ricardo replied.

"How did you know about us?" Lyn asked.

"I arrived a few minutes ago and read each of your passports. I see all of you are very well traveled."

"Yes," answered Rid. "Both for business and pleasure. This is my first time in Ethiopia, however."

"Hopefully you will find it to your liking. We don't have many first-class tourist facilities, but the sights are spectacular and the people are friendly."

They paused to order that night's special, roast leg of lamb with served with couscous. Then Rid said, "Hakeem, what can you tell us about the murders?"

"A nasty affair. The Furhwerks were staying in their tent at the dig site. Apparently they wanted to work late that night. Most nights they came in to town to stay here, as it gets quite cold at night in the desert. Anyway, from what we have pieced together, they must have been awakened by robbers, who were taking artifacts from the main tent. The robbers had already killed the lone sentry. When Mr. Fuhrwerk came out of his tent to see what was going on, the robbers spotted him and killed them both. The autopsies revealed Mrs. Fuhrwerk had been raped three times before she was killed."

"Oh my God!" Lyn uttered. "How awful."

"Yes," the detective went on. "Neither of them were a pretty sight. They were killed by multiple stab wounds by more than one curved dagger. The kind most commonly found in India."

"That's curious," Rid interrupted. "So you think it could be three people from India?"

"That's one theory. But passport control doesn't show any recent visitors from India. They could have driven in from the Sudan. There are a number of border crossings that are unmanned."

"What about the artifacts?" Ricardo wanted to know.

"From the Fuhrwerks' records, we think they took one small statue of what appears to be an early Christian carving, several pieces of broken pottery which had been numbered for assembly, and several old coins, safety pins, and other assorted small items."

"Was there any evidence that there may have been jewels or gold there?" Rid asked.

"The experts at our National Museum said nothing like that had been retrieved from that site. They had discussed on a number of occasions with the Fuhrwerks their speculation that this could be the site of the legendary King, Prester John."

"And what do they think about that?" the Monsignor asked.

"They think it is unlikely as there is little water supply at the site. They tell me this mythical king had a very large court that couldn't exist without water."

"I'd like to visit with the museum experts, if I may," Ricardo said.

"I can set that up for you," Hakeem offered. "How is ten tomorrow morning?"

"That's fine. I'll be there."

"Ask for Ethna Nuala. She's in charge of the Furhwerks' site."

As they finished dinner, the talk turned to modern Ethiopia and the need for foreign investment. The rebellion in the early 1990s had cut off most funds. Tourism was increasing, though, so two new hotels were under construction. Then the detective excused himself saying he had to be back at headquarters by ten. After he left, Rid summarized. "Really, we gained a great deal of information. The Christian statue must have excited the Fuhrwerks. And the Indian daggers. I don't know what to make of that."

"Mary's rape means these were really bad thugs," Lyn added.

"Yes. I will pray for their souls tonight," Corso said.

"Thank you, Ricardo," Lyn replied.

"And the bit about the lack of water in the desert. I wonder if they're talking about now, or what this was like in the twelfth century. I will ask Ms. Nuala when I see her tomorrow." the Priest suggested.

"What about you, Lyn? You didn't ask about the library." Rid asked.

"The front desk can give me directions. I didn't want to overemphasize our interest in Prester John."

"Good thinking. We can't be sure who is to be trusted, although I feel good about our policeman," Rid suggested.

"I have a funny feeling that we were being watched throughout dinner," Clark offered.

"I'm bothered very much by the robbers being from India," Rid speculated. "If that's true, then they were probably sent here to murder the Fuhrwerks and the robbery was just a cover-up."

"If that's the case, you better get Hakeem to go with you two to the site tomorrow," Lyn said.

"I'll call him. Everyone knows their assignment?" Rid asked.

"Yes," came the unanimous reply.

When they all returned to their beds, each, like the team in Venice, had a sense of foreboding about someone else seeking Prester John.

EIGHT

Ethiopia

Both groups were active early the next morning. Rid had called Hakeem Olajoni the night before and he suggested they use his police off-road vehicle and driver. He would pick up Rid and Clark at 7 AM to beat the heat of the day. Rid then called Clark and woke him up to give him the early start news. He also called the desk to cancel the car he had reserved.

The trip out to the dig site took about an hour. After leaving Addis Ababa the road wound through some small rolling hills and then onto a flat desert where the road became a track in the sand. When they arrived at the site, there was a small oasis nearby. Olajoni said the water was safe to drink, but the group decided to stick with the bottled water from the hotel. There were two guards at the entrance to the small, fenced-off area.

"Let me give you a short tour," said Olajoni. "Then you can wander around as much as you like."

He showed them the main dig, where small foundations outlined what may have once been a building larger than a house. Next, they looked at the work tables, where there were still a number of artifacts and broken jars. Then they went to the tent where the Fuhrwerks were murdered. It had been thoroughly cleaned, so there was nothing there of interest.

"I'd like to go back to the work area. I wonder why they only took the one statue," Rid said.

"Some of these were probably found after the robbery," Clark surmised.

"No," said Captain Olajoni. "We have had this site closed since the murders."

"Then, it is curious, isn't it?" Rid said to Hakeem.

"Yes. We had the same question. Remember, I told you it may have been a Christian statue. All of the ones left here are local tribal or Moslem. We believe the robbers knew what they were looking for," Hakeem explained.

"It's almost like they were trying to hide the fact that a Christian statue was here," Rid said.

"That could be," Keene added.

At that moment, a jeep came over the small rise on the other side of the oasis. One person was driving, and two passengers had automatic weapons in their hands. They began firing at the guards at the entrance, several hundred yards away. One of the guards fell, and the other jumped into the guard house.

"Let's get out of here," Hakeem yelled as they all dashed for his four-by-four.

They sped away from the gate and the approaching intruders. They crashed through a weak part of the fence into the open desert. The jeep circled the camp and started to follow. The men in the black suits were too far behind for their gunfire to be effective.

The four-by-four simply had too much power for the jeep. Eventually, they were able to turn toward Addis Ababa. They arrived at the hotel without further contact with the jeep.

Rid asked, "Any idea who that was, Hakeem?"

"No. They must be the robbers who are still watching the site," he replied.

"I agree. But why?" Rid pushed on.

"I don't know. It's like they are protecting the site. They must not want something discovered," the policeman said.

"I think we need to find out who they are," Clark suggested.

"I'll organize a search party for this afternoon. I can get a unit from the army. And planes to locate them from the air," Olajoni offered.

"Good. I want to go with you," Rid said. "Clark, you stay here at the hotel and brief Lyn and Father Corso when they return from their visits to the Museum and Library. Let's go, Hakeem."

Clark relayed the story of the morning to Ricardo and Lyn over lunch.

"A most curious turn of events," the Monsignor said.

"Yes," agreed Lyn. "It's like in the movies where some group has promised to guard a tomb forever."

"There are such sects in India. And that may account for the curved daggers," Clark added.

"The mystery deepens," Ricardo replied.

NINE

Venice

Milt Young and the Byerlys were standing in the portico of the side door of San Georgio Church when Father Saputo arrived to open the Library for them. By about 12:30, Milt and the Byerlys finished their reading of Marco Polo's notes. They continued to be impressed with the precise detail of his writing. Although the notes were full of new wonders to Polo, he balanced his awe of them with good descriptions of the people and everyday life around Peiping and Kublai Khan's Imperial City. He searched for over two years for Prester John's Court. Finally he found some ruins of a large house of worship. It had produced both Buddhist and early Christian symbols. Most notably, Polo found a mosaic of the Christian fish on the floor. He was convinced this was Prester John's palace.

"I really believe this is the site," JoAnna said.

"Me, too," Reggie agreed.

"I agree. I think Marco Polo was on the right track. I wonder if anyone has worked the site since then?" Milt pondered. "We'll find out when we apply to the Chinese Bureau of Antiquities for a permit to go there."

"Can we go?" Jo said excitedly.

"I don't see why not," Milt answered.

"Somebody did kill the Fuhrwerks," Reggie reminded the other two.

"Yes," replied Milt, "I'm betting they're connected to whoever is showing up here at two o'clock."

"You're probably right," Jo said.

"You two go have lunch with the Countess and tell her what we have found. I'm going to station myself down by those gondolas, where I can see this door."

Milt waited and watched. Just after 2 PM, two men disembarked from the Vaporetto that came from the Santa Lucia train station. They wore dark suits and ties and looked like they came from India, Pakistan, or Afghanistan. One wore a small turban with some kind of metal shield holding it together in the front. Father Saputo welcomed them to San Georgio. Before he led them inside to the Church Library, he glanced around the square and spotted Young. He gave no signal of recognition.

Milt decided to wait until they came out. He didn't have to wait long. They left the church only twenty minutes after they arrived. They seemed in a hurry and jumped aboard a Vaporetto that was just leaving for the station. The turban was missing. Milt decided to go into the church to see what they were after. He found Father Saputo in the hall outside the Library. He was lying on the floor, oozing blood from a stab wound in his side.

"Thank God you are here. Help me," he whispered to Milt.

"Here, take my coat, Press it on the wound to stop the bleeding, while I go for help." Milt said as he folded his jacket into a tight compress.

He ran into the church and found a sextant cleaning the confessional booths. Milt's Italian had become proficient because of living in Rome. He explained that Father Saputo had been stabbed and it was urgent they get medical attention. The sextant ran for the main Church Office. Milt returned to Saputo.

"Can you tell me what happened, Cesar?" Milt asked.

"They were not as interested in Marco Polo's notes as they were about who you were and why you were here. When I refused to tell them who you are, they started to hit me. I once was an amateur boxer, so I started to fight back. Then one of them came at me with a knife. It was one of those long, curved daggers like you see in Turkey. I avoided his first thrust and knocked his turban to the floor. He caught me with his second thrust and I let out a loud scream, even though I knew it was unlikely anyone would hear. They ran out and I crawled out of the library to here when you arrived."

"Help is on the way," Milt said as he took over holding the compress on the wound. Five minutes later, a water ambulance with emergency medical technicians arrived and they immediately began giving the priest blood. The Bishop of San Georgio had also arrived in the hallway. He began praying for Father Saputo.

After they had loaded Cesar on the ambulance boat, they used their siren to clear a path up the Grand Canal to the hospital. The Bishop invited Milt into the church to tell him what had happened. Milt related the story about the mysterious visitors who could have been there looking for him. He told of the fight and stabbing,

He also explained about the turban. "The police will want that turban. I would like to have a look at it before they get here."

"Yes. I'd like to survey the library," the Bishop said as he rose from his chair.

The two of them went back to the library. It was obvious that a scuffle had taken place. Tables and chairs had been turned over and books had fallen from their shelves.

"Don't move or touch anything, Bishop. The police will want it as it is," Milt admonished.

"All right. There is the turban," the cleric said pointing to it behind a table by the file cabinets.

Milt didn't touch the turban, but he got down on the floor so he could study the badge. "It's oval in shape," he described. "It's bronze, I think. There is a picture of a curved dagger down the middle. On the left from top to bottom are the initials D.P., and on the right, the initials are F.J. Mean anything to you, Father?"

"No. I hear the police launch coming," he responded.

The police showed up in force. There must have been twenty of them. They cordoned off the church and let no one in or out. A team of forensic specialists began work in the library, looking for fingerprints or other clues. They took great interest in the turban. When they asked Milt to tell them what he knew, he recounted every detail. When he reached the part about them jumping the Vaporetto to the station, the Captain in charge radioed the police on watch at Santa Lucia.

"Perhaps we will be in time to catch them," the Captain said. "Here is my card, Mr. Young. If you think of anything else, please call me."

The card read "Captain Antonio Philipelli, Policia de Venizia," with a phone number and address below.

"May I go now?" Milt asked,

"Yes, but please stay in Venice until we have a chance to talk to Father Saputo. You may be able to fill in some details or resolve conflicts in his and your stories," Captain Philipelli ordered.

"I'm staying at the Savoia," Milt said.

The Captain told one of his men to escort Milt out so he could get through the police line. When he reached the hotel, the Byerlys were not there. "Probably shopping." Milt thought. He went to the Danieli and found the Countess with the Byerlys, having tea in the main salon. Milt joined them and rapidly told them of the assault on Cesar.

"I hope he makes it. I like him," JoAnna said.

"We all do," Reggie added.

"What about this turban you described?" the Countess asked. "You said there was an emblem on the front?"

"Yes. It was oval, made of bronze, and had a curved dagger down the middle. On the left side of the dagger were the initials

D.P. from top to bottom. On the right, the initials F.J. with the F on top," Milt described.

"Have you tried reading them across?" Liesel said with a coy smile.

"You get D.F. across the top and P.J. on the bottom," Reggie said.

"Bingo!" the Countess grinned.

"The P.J. must stand for Prester John," Jo screeched.

"No doubt," said Milt. "But who are these guys, and what's the D.F. mean?"

"Another unsolved mystery," Reggie stated.

"You three go on with your cocktails. Excuse me, your tea. I need to call Rid to tell him about this and to see what they have found," Milt said as he left the salon.

Back in his room, he put through the call to Rid in Addis Ababa. The hotel operator said she would ring him back when the call went through. Twenty minutes later, the phone rang.

"Wait till you hear what happened to us," Rid yelled into the phone.

"We have a story to tell, too," Milt replied, "You first, Rid."

Rid relayed the incidents of the day, including the shootings and chase by three thugs that looked Indian. He finished by telling Milt there was no sign of them when they searched later in the afternoon. "It's like they disappeared in the desert," he said.

"Were they wearing black suits and ties?" Milt wanted to know.

"Yeah! I thought that was strange in the desert. How did you know?"

"Ours were dressed the same. They stabbed the Priest at San Georgio with a curved dagger."

"That's the weapon that killed the Fuhrwerks," Rid said more excitedly.

"One of ours lost his turban. It had an emblem on it of a curved dagger and the letters D.F. and P.J.," Milt said.

"We know what the P.J. is, I'll bet. But what's this D.F.?" Rid pondered.

"I don't know yet. We better find out, though, before we probe much further. It's getting dangerous on this treasure hunt," Milt said before he hung up the phone.

Both of the principals of Janus International, one in Italy and one in Ethiopia, described for their board members the events of the day in both locations. Each closed their story with a similar line. "It is obvious there is a group intent on keeping us from finding Prester John. It's far too dangerous for any of you to continue. Make plans to return to Rome and from there to your homes. We'll keep you posted on our search."

"I wonder if Professor O'Brien knew about these villains and if that's why he hired us?" Clark asked.

"That could be," Rid replied, "When you get back to Maine, you can brief him on everything, including the initials. See what he says and call me."

None of those in Addis Ababa or Venice slept well that night. Each had visions of someone sneaking into their room with a large curved dagger held above their heart.

TEN

Paris

The same day the Janus groups had their problems in Ethiopia and Venice, a meeting was held in Paris to organize a holding company named EPIC. The acronym stood for Energy Producers International Corporation. They were meeting in the ballroom of the George V Hotel, There were over 100 people there from across the globe. Heads of private power companies and government managers of public power producers. The self-appointed CEO of EPIC walked to the podium.

"Good morning! Thank you for coming. I am Johnathan Presterman, CEO of EPIC. I believe you will find today's presentation both stimulating and exciting. Great changes are occurring in the power industry, as evidenced by the recent failure of Enron, a longtime big player. The current recession has caused two governments, Taiwan and Indonesia, to privatize their state-owned power operations. EPIC was the successful bidder in both cases. We also own a portion of the franchise for power in Brazil, and we are currently in discussion with three U.S. companies, two private and one municipally owned. In Europe we are talking with Russia who is strapped for cash about a buy out of all their plants. That's a very large purchase and, frankly, one beyond our resources. That's why you are here. EPIC is prepared to offer up to 49 percent of its shares to you at an initial offering total price of $15 billion. It can be for one of you, a consortium of several of you; or, as I would prefer, from all of you on a pro-rata basis by your kilowatts produced over the last three years. By joining together in this effort to consolidate the weaker producers under one umbrella, we will improve their reliability, provide a stronger network grid for using excess capacity, and allow power to be shifted geographically to where it is most needed. As owners of shares in EPIC, you will receive discounted prices on any power you buy and premium prices on any you have for sale. A true win-win situation. Our vision and long-range plan is to own or share enough of the world's power capacity that we can dictate pricing. In fact, if we have a large enough piece, we can control the world's economy and ensure continued growth well into this new century. I could go on, but let me stop here to take your questions."

A representative of Amgen Power in St. Louis rose. "What if all of us don't want to participate? If a certain percentage goes along, is it still a go?"

"I set a target of two-thirds of the kilowatts represented here as a minimum. Having read your most recent annual reports, that would give us enough to do the Russian deal."

"Who will govern EPIC?" a German executive wanted to know.

"Like any corporation, the shareholders will elect a board of directors at each annual meeting. That board would, in turn, elect the senior management."

The German pushed on. "You control 51 percent of the stock, so you can elect a Board that has no minority interest representation."

"I meant to say that I plan a board of eighteen, including myself The other seventeen would be nine majority and eight minority nominees."

"What are the capabilities of your management team?" the Commissioner of Egypt Power asked.

"They all have over ten years' experience in leadership roles in power producers. This is another benefit of belonging to EPIC. We will build a pool of superior talent that can either be hired or rented by you. If we acquire a company with weak management, we'll draw on the pool to provide new leadership."

"Where is EPIC's headquarters?" from the Peruvian attendee.

"I have been living in Brazil the last two years to be close to our negotiations there. We will, however, need to be constantly in the financial markets, so I plan to move our headquarters to New York within the next six months."

The questions continued for about another twenty minutes. The final one was, perhaps, the most difficult. It came from the Chief Financial Officer of Florida Power & Light. "Do we have to buy in with cash or can we trade some of our shares for EPIC?"

"The reason I suggested cash was to complete the Russian acquisition as quickly as possible. But shares of good financially-rated companies would certainly be welcome. It would add to our worldwide grid, and we can use those shares as collateral for any needed Russian loan."

"What if it doesn't raise enough?" the Japanese delegate asked.

"I am working on a project that could provide an unlimited supply of capital. I must keep it secret for now, and it may not work out. But, if it does, EPIC will be the richest company on earth. Now, it's time for lunch. We have cocktails waiting in the foyer and a buffet set up in the next room. I will be circulating around throughout cocktails and lunch if any of you have individual questions. After lunch, there will be packets available to each of you, detailing EPIC's plan of operation, our current financials, management biographies, a transcript of today's meeting, and a calculation of what share each of you would own if we got 100 percent participation. From that you can make calculations of what your cost would be if we don't get 100 percent. For example, if we got 75 percent, you would increase your share by one-third. Let's adjourn for lunch," Presterman closed the meeting.

A number of the executives present expressed interest in the plan. Many others had questions specifically related to their local situations. Presterman was careful to answer everyone to their satisfaction. The meeting, cocktails, and lunch were all being videotaped for his later use.

When the lunch was over, Presterman went up to his suite feeling very good about the events of the day. There was an e-mail message on his portable computer. It read, "Call me. It's about the search." It was signed Randy. Presterman knew it was just 9 A.M. in Maine, but he dialed the Professor's office phone.

"O'Brien here," he answered.

"It's Presterman. What's going on?"

"I have had reports from my contacts in Venice, a policeman, and Addis Ababa, a hotel clerk, that both of the Janus teams ran into difficulty today. In both cases they were attacked by Arabs or Indians who all wore black suits and carried long, curved daggers."

"Not of my doing," Presterman answered.

"Nor mine. I thought you might know who they are as you have been studying Prester John for some time," O'Brien suggested.

"I saw a minor reference somewhere, that a sect of Hindus from India had converted to Christianity. Let me think. Why the connection? Oh yes, they called themselves 'The Defenders of the Faith of Prester John.' But that reference was for several centuries ago."

"Do you suppose they could still be active, Johnathan?"

"If they are, they could scare off our treasure hunters. You should get a call soon from Clark Keene. See what he says about their attackers. Then suggest you will look into it and, a day later, give them the name of the Defenders of the Faith of Prester John."

"All right, Mr. Presterman. I'll contact you after I've heard from Janus," O'Brien said. To himself he was thinking, 'I wonder what your name really is, Mr. Presterman?"

ELEVEN

Venice

Captain Philipelli of the Venice Police called Milt Young at 8 AM.

"You are free to leave the city, Mr. Young. Father Saputo is doing well. He told us what happened and how you saved his life."

"His own strength is what saved him. May I visit him in the hospital?" Milt asked.

"Certainly. After eleven this morning. Is that all right?" the policeman suggested.

"Yes. I will book our party on a late afternoon flight back to Rome," Milt said.

"Thank you for your help, Mr. Young. Arrivederci."

"Arrivederci, Captain."

Over breakfast, Milt told Reggie and JoAnna Byerly about the call from Philipelli about Father Saputo's improved condition. "I'm going to see him later this morning. I want to tell him about the initials on the turban to see if he has any knowledge of what they may mean."

"Let me show you something else that may be of interest," Reggie said. "I went out early this morning and bought a *Herald American* newspaper. Look at this article in the financial section."

He handed the paper to Milt. The article's headline read, EPIC PROPOSES WORLDWIDE ELECTRIC UTILITY. The story covered the meeting in Paris and suggested that EPIC was trying to build a financial base of strong utility companies as investors to jointly acquire troubled companies to build a worldwide grid of power. The line that caught Milt's eye was the one that caused Reggie to suggest he read the article. It said, "The meeting was hosted at Paris's George V by Brazilian financier Johnathan Presterman. It was by invitation only, so no details are yet available."

"Our anonymous backer, you think?" Milt queried.

"It sure could be," JoAnna answered. "His name is so close to Prester John."

"I think it's him," Reggie added. "If it is him, then I would bet that Johnathan Presterman is an assumed name."

"You're probably right. We will have to see what we can find out about this Presterman and EPIC," Milt said. "I'm going to get tickets for us on a mid-afternoon flight to Rome. I'll talk to the Countess, but I believe she wants to stay here a few more days and then fly back to Corfu."

"We'll go pack. And I have some last-minute shopping to do," Jo said.

"She's buying some Venetian glass accent pieces for the school. Including a chandelier for our entry foyer," Reggie explained.

Milt suggested, "Let's meet at San Trovaso for lunch at one. You bring Liesel. I'll come from the hospital. Then we'll have time to take a water taxi to the airport. Now, let's go pack."

While they packed, they each kept thinking to themselves, "Who is this Johnathan Presterman?"

TWELVE

Ethiopia

Monsignor Corso and Lyn were telling Ridley and Clark about their contacts the day before. The shooting and chase, plus the call from Milt Young in Venice about similar men in black suits with curved daggers, had dominated the conversation the night before. They were seated in a private booth in the breakfast room where they could talk freely.

"It's no mere coincidence that both our teams ran into the same bad guys," Rid said. "We must find out who they are. I also want to know if our anonymous employer is connected to them."

"What did you say Milt called them from the initials on the turban in Venice?" Clark asked.

"The initials are D.F. and P.J.," Rid replied. "We think the P.J. must stand for Prester John. The D.F. is still unknown."

"I'd say let's check our Vatican records. We may have a reference to this group," Father Ricardo offered.

"Good idea, Ricardo. We'll do that when we get back to Rome. I have the desk clerk working on our tickets now for the noon flight back. First, though, I want to hear about your day yesterday. Lyn, you first. Then Ricardo."

Lyn began, "I spent about six hours at the National Library. They had very little on Prester John. They did have one copy of the Silverman book I told you about. The most significant thing I found were two news items from old papers. One from the 1880s about a Dutch team digging at the desert site of an old temple. The article was written as they started their dig. I could find no reports on what they found. The second article was from 1922. It also reported on a dig at the site. This effort was funded by an English lord, William Floyd, who hired a number of noted archeologists, including the famous Dr. Stanley Ikenberry, to find the temple of Prester John."

"Whoa! Do you think this Lord Floyd could be related to the Sir Dean Floyd that was involved in our last case?" Rid asked.

I guess it could have been his father or grandfather," Lyn continued. "In any event, the article said they found no evidence of a large enough construction site to hold a palace such as Prester John described in his letter to Manuel I. After about eighteen months they gave up the search and went home."

"I can add a little to that," Corso said. "My visit to the National Museum was very interesting, although not extremely fruitful. Ethna Nuala, who oversees this site, turned out to be a very bright Irish lass who came to Ethiopia during the famine relief effort and then stayed. She had records about and artifacts from the Ikenberry expedition. I looked at them. Not much of importance. Earthenware mostly. There was a log of the activity, in which Ikenberry speculated that there were some old maps at the site. But none were ever found, or he took them and never reported it to the museum. Ms. Nuala also showed me everything from the Fuhrwerks' dig. It matched what you found out at the site. More earthenware, pins, needles, some flints for fire starting. Curiously, there were no weapons. It must have been a peaceful place. Finally, the staff at the museum say that the site has always been short on water. All there has been is the oasis next to the site. They have records back over 300 years about travelers stopping there. So my best guess is this is not Prester John's court. Perhaps he visited here on his way to India or China."

"A very interesting possibility," Clark said.

The desk clerk came to their table to tell Rid he had an overseas phone call that he could take in the booth in the lobby. Rid asked the others to wait while he took the call.

"Hello," said Taylor, as he picked up the phone.

"Hi, Rid, anything new there?" Milt questioned.

"No further sign of the bad guys. They just vanished in the desert. But a great deal of corroboration that this is not the Prester's place," Rid replied. "How about you?"

"Not much. The Priest from San Georgio is recovering nicely. I saw him this morning. I asked him if the initials from the turban meant anything to him. He said he had never heard of them," Milt explained. "We're going back to Rome this afternoon."

"We are, too. Ricardo thinks he may find something on these initials in the Vatican Library. Oh, I almost forgot. The sponsor of a dig at this site in the 1920s was an English lord named William Floyd," Rid said.

"Are you thinking what I'm thinking?" Milt replied.

"We think it must be Dean Floyd's father or grandfather. Do you think he could be our sponsor?" Rid queried.

"It would explain why he wants to be anonymous. But there is another possibility. Reggie found a piece in the financial section of today's *Herald American* about a power company executive who is trying to take control of the electric generating industry. His name, if you can believe it, is Johnathan Presterman."

"You're kidding, Milt."

"No. I saw the article, Rid."

"Maybe this Johnathan Presterman and our Dean Floyd are one and the same," Rid speculated.

"Maybe. We'll talk more about it tomorrow at the office," Milt closed.

"See you there," Rid said as he hung up.

Rid returned to the table and reported on the call to the Monsignor and the Keenes. They were excited at the thought than Johnathan Presterman might be an alias for Dean Floyd, whom Ridley, Milt, and the Byerlys foiled in his attempt to take over the world's military.

"This control of electric generation sounds like a scheme Floyd would attempt," Clark said.

"Control the world's power and you control the world," Rid uttered as he rose from the table.

THIRTEEN

Rome

The next morning, the two teams met at Janus International's office. They again reviewed the events in Ethiopia and Venice. They reaffirmed that the two sets of attackers were connected.

"How could they know we were going to these two places?" Lyn asked.

"Yeah. How could they have known Janus was involved at all?" JoAnna added.

Clark said "The only person besides us who knew where we were going is Professor O'Brien."

"That makes no sense," Ridley replied. "He hired us to find the treasure. Why would he send assassins to stop us?"

"You're right. There must be another explanation," Milt added. "Maybe they have local contacts in every locale related to Prester John."

"Could be. They must use phone taps as well. That's the only way they could get to us so soon after we arrived at Addis Ababa and Venice," Reggie suggested.

"They will probably show up here before too long and try to put some listening devices in here," Milt said.

They all looked around the room. JoAnna said, "Looks like they have already been here." She was holding a table lamp upside down and there was a small disc glued to bottom.

"Milt, get our bug finder. Let's hold the conversation until he has swept the offices."

While Milt found four more bugs, Rid wrote a script for all of them. Milt laid the devices on the conference table. Rid pointed to them and to his ear. He then read from the script, "I think this search may be too dangerous. Perhaps we should back out and refund the unused expense money."

"We certainly don't want to put you and Milt in danger," Lyn read.

"Reggie and I agree," JoAnna followed. 'Besides we really haven't been able to locate Prester John's court."

"It is a complicated case. One I normally would be eager to pursue. I'm not worried about danger for myself But these people would know who all of you are if they picked up one of our brochures when they were here," Milt stated.

"If you are listening," Rid said to the bugs, "We have found your five devices. Very sophisticated. But you no longer need to oppose us, as we are withdrawing from the search."

After that they all walked outside at Rid's urging.

"Are we really going to quit?" Clark asked.

"Of course not," Rid and Milt said in unison.

Milt added, "We will be more careful about our plans in the future, now that we know they are watching."

"Maybe Ricardo will solve the mystery of the initials," Rid hoped. "He asked me to call him this afternoon."

"Is there anything more for us to do?" JoAnna asked.

"No. You should make your arrangements to fly back to England tomorrow," Rid said. "Keenes, you should do the same for your flight to Boston, When you get back to Maine, I still want you to meet with the Professor and bring him up to date. I'm most interested in his reaction to the initials."

"I'll call you after I talk to O'Brien," Clark said.

"Better use e-mail in case we get new bugs," Milt said. "In fact, that should be our standard method of communicating until this affair is over."

"Okay," everyone agreed.

"Goodbye, then. You are a great bunch of directors," Milt said.

"We appreciate your support and your analytical abilities," Rid added.

After they were gone, Milt and Rid discussed their next moves.

"Let's wait a few days to see if things cool off. If there are no more bugging attempts, or if Ricardo or the Keenes solve the riddle of the initials, we can pick up the trail of Prester John," Rid said.

"We should also see if we can find any more on Johnathan Presterman. I sure would like to see a picture of him," Milt added.

"Good thinking," Rid replied. "Prester John and Johnathan Presterman. Wonder if they're related?"

"I'd bet on that." Milt said with a grin.

FOURTEEN

Rome

Three days later, Ridley and Milt were sitting in their offices, waiting for a call from Clark. The phone rang and they both picked up.

"Hi. It's Clark. My e-mail is down, but I have the answer to the initials!" he opened excitedly.

"Tell us," Milt said eagerly. "I checked for phone bugs this morning."

"When I talked to Professor O'Brien yesterday afternoon, he asked me to let him do a little research. He called back early this morning, and we met at a local breakfast place. He says the initials stand for 'Defenders of the Faith of Prester John.' He also knew something about them. He said they were a sect of Hindus who had converted to Christianity in the fourteenth century. This was about 200 years after P.J.'s letter to Byzantium. The Professor said the group took a blood oath to keep the faith of Prester John alive and to protect his treasure, even though they didn't know where it was."

"That's 600 years ago. Did he have anything more current?" Rid asked.

"No. He said they haven't been heard from very often since. Apparently, there was some interference with the Floyd expedition in the 1920s, but it was attributed to people unknown," Clark replied.

"I wonder if Marco Polo ran into them in China?" Rid questioned.

"We didn't find any reference to them in his notes. He was too early, anyway," Milt responded.

"What did you think of the Professor's reaction to our attacks, Clark?" Ridley wanted to know.

"Very little. It was almost like he already knew about them. And I think he already had this stuff on the Defenders of the Faith. He just stalled me over night to give the impression he looked it up."

"That is very possible. Ricardo has found no reference to them in the Vatican Library," Milt said. He went on. "Did you ask O'Brien about Johnathan Presterman?"

"Yes, in a way. I showed him a copy of the news article and asked if he had seen it?

"He glanced at it and said, 'Look at this name. It's similar to our Prester John. But I don't know him.' He could have been telling the truth or lying. He was hard to read on this question. My gut feeling is that Johnathan Presterman is his anonymous backer."

"He almost has to be," Rid began. "And I'm betting he is really Dean Floyd. Everything points that way. First is the similarity of names. Second, Dean Floyd would hide his identity because he is still wanted for treason in England. He also would want to stay anonymous from us as we know him. And finally, his father or grandfather sought Prester John in the 1920s. Pretty overwhelming coincidences, wouldn't you say?"

"I'll say," Clark replied.

"Plus he may have added information or maps from the Ikenberry dig in Ethiopia." Milt said. "Didn't the person at the museum in Addis Ababa tell our Monsignor there was a rumor of some found maps?"

"Yes, she did," Rid said.

"And, you can add to your list of coincidences this Presterman's scheme for world domination of the electric power industry. That certainly smacks of Dean Floyd."

"Right, we still need to have a financial research study done on his company, EPIC," Rid went on.

"I can look it up on the Internet," Milt offered.

"Go for it," Rid said. "Goodbye, Clark. Glad you and Lyn made it home safe. We'll call you in a few days to give a progress report."

By the time Rid got off the phone, Milt was sitting at his computer looking at a screen that read, "EPIC—Energy Producers International Corporation."

Milt began to read, "It says it was founded and incorporated in Brazil two years ago by Johnathan Presterman."

"That fits with when Floyd escaped from us in England. I remember him saying, 'I'll be back.' But I guess I didn't expect him so soon. What else does it say, Milt?"

"It says their shares are traded over the counter. They have applied for listing on most of the world's major stock exchanges. The New York, Tokyo, London, Frankfurt, and Swiss markets. Then there is a history section that tells of their acquisition of the Taiwan and Indonesian governments' power plants followed by a description of their planned acquisition in Brazil. There is a brief reference to his plan to get other power companies to invest in acquiring other government-owned and private electric generating operations. The rest of the page is their financial results. They have grown very rapidly in their first two years. Over $1 billion in revenues in their second year."

"Impressive. I wonder why he wants us to find Prester John's treasure if he is having that kind of success?" Rid spoke his thought out loud.

"Probably to move faster. At some point trade organizations will become nervous about someone controlling too much of the power industry. Governments would stop approving their acquisition requests."

Rid said, "That's another good reason for his inviting other strong utilities in as shareholders. If they move quickly, they could control enough to dictate their own terms of government approval."

"Scary, isn't it?" Milt replied. "There are no pictures of Johnathan Presterman. It just says he emigrated to Brazil from France and he is a wealthy financier. It does fit his organizing board. Looks like they are all lawyers from major cities of the world. It says that once they are listed on the exchanges, they will organize a more permanent board of international business leaders."

"No help there," Rid said. "I told the Monsignor I would meet him for lunch today at the Vatican dining room to bring him up to date. You want to go?"

"Yes, we can see if he has looked any further in the library for references to the Defenders of the Faith of Prester John."

"It's really unbelievable that they could still be active after over 600 years," Rid pondered.

"We have dead bodies and a stabbed priest to prove it. And they know who we are," Milt expressed.

Rid ended their session with, "Now that is a scary thought!"

FIFTEEN

Rome

Monsignor Corso was very interested in Milt and Ridley's report. Particularly the identification of the Defenders of the Faith of Prester John.

"I've seen references to other Defenders of the Faith groups in our library. But none related to Prester John. I'll have the staff look again," Ricardo said. "Tell me more about this Johnathan Presterman."

Rid presented the facts and coincidences that convinced the Janus duo that their employer was really Dean Floyd. Corso agreed.

"Where are you two going next?" he asked.

Milt replied, "China, to follow Marco Polo's trail. That is, if we get permission from the Chinese government."

"I can help with that. The Vatican is not without influence, even in China. They have a legation here in Rome. I should be able to get you a visa there. What should I use as your reason?" Ricardo offered.

"Put down we're doing research for a book about Marco Polo and want to follow his notes," Milt suggested.

"That's good," Rid agreed.

They finished their lunch in the Vatican dining room and returned to the office. As they approached the door, they saw that it was partly open. There were muffled voices in a foreign language inside.

"I'm not carrying my PPK," Milt whispered.

"Me neither," answered Rid. "Let's call 911 for backup."

Milt used his cell phone to call the police. They waited about five minutes.

The police had not arrived, but they heard the people inside coming toward the door.

"Quick, take a position beside the door. We'll surprise them as they come out," Rid pointed to the opposite side from where he was standing.

As two men in black suits with black ties came through the door, Rid and Milt jumped them from behind. Rid knocked his man over and lit on top of him. The assailant was very quick and very strong. He broke Rid's choke hold and rolled away. He was pulling his dagger when Rid smashed the heel of his hand into the tip of his nose, driving the bone into his brain. As he was dying, the last thrust of his knife caught Ridley's left forearm, making a four-inch gash.

Milt's opponent was larger. He bounced away from Milt and moved several steps down the hall. He turned, drew his curved dagger, and started back toward Milt. Loud sirens indicated the police were arriving. So the second intruder turned and ran out the back of the building. Milt stayed with Rid and put a tourniquet around his injured arm. The police came running down the hall.

"It's over. You can put your guns away," Milt shouted.

"What happened?" the squad leader asked.

Milt told the story about finding them inside their office, the fight, Rid's stabbing, and the one that escaped through the back door. Two of the policemen went out the back to check, but found nothing. Another called for an ambulance for Rid. It arrived a few minutes later. They took him to the hospital where they said would need quite a few stitches.

The police asked Milt to check their offices to see if anything was missing. He found four more listening devices but didn't see that anything was taken. After dusting for fingerprints, the police left.

Two hours later, Rid returned. Milt told him about the new bugs.

"I didn't see anything missing," he said.

"What about the piece of paper that was on my desk?" Rid said while he opened his desk drawer with his good arm.

"What was on it, Rid?"

"Our reasons for suspecting that Johnathan Presterman is the sponsor of our search for Prester John."

"Having seen how the so-called Defenders work, I don't think Floyd, a.k.a. Presterman, will remain anonymous for long," Milt suggested. "Now let's get you home so you can rest."

SIXTEEN

Rome

The next morning, Monsignor Corso called the Janus office. Ridley answered the phone, "Janus International."

"It's Ricardo, Rid. Milt told me about the intruders. How is your arm?"

"It's okay. The cut's not that deep. Thanks for your concern," Rid replied.

The Curator went on, "I have you all set up to meet with the Chinese legation today at 3 PM. They will ask you about your trip to do research on Marco Polo. They will be incredibly slow, but they have said they will grant you the visas."

"Where are they?"

"It's off the Via Veneto at 16 Via Aurora," Ricardo said.

Rid answered, "I know that street. We go there to Marcello's a lot."

"Good luck."

"Thanks for your help, Ricardo."

Rid told his partner that the Vatican had arranged for their visas, but that they would have to go through the application process. That afternoon, they arrived at the Chinese Legation ahead of the appointment time. They were ushered into a small office that was cluttered with files and loose papers.

"Welcome to China. I am Den Ling Du. What can I do for you?"

"We have come to get visitor visas for a trip to China," Rid said. "I believe you had a call from the Vatican about our trip."

"Ah, yes. But these things take time. All these papers are requests for either travel or doing business in China. What is the purpose of your trip?"

"We are writing a book about Marco Polo. We want to see the places he went," Milt answered.

"Do you plan to take any antiquities away from China?"

'No, we would turn over to your government any relics we might find," Rid replied.

"How long do you plan to stay?" the bureaucrat asked.

"We're not certain. It shouldn't be longer that the thirty days your visa application is for," Rid said as he read from the application.

"Please to show me your passports. Do you have any extra passport style pictures?"

They handed over the extra pictures they knew would be needed and their passports. Rid's was from the United States and Milt's from Great Britain. The legation officer studied them for a few minutes, looking at all the entry stamps from around the world, "You are well traveled, with many countries' visas already recorded. Does your writing of books cause you to travel so much?"

"We also travel for pleasure, and we work as advisors to corporations about preparing histories of their companies," Rid explained.

"I must go in the other room to do some processing. Please, wait here," the official said.

After he left, Milt raised one finger from his hand that was flat on the table. He was pointing at a large mirror set in the far wall. They had both seen enough of these from both sides to know it was one-way glass and that someone in the next room had been watching. They sat silently and did not try to look at any of the papers. After about twenty minutes, the Chinese official returned.

"Here are your passports, with Chinese visas inside. We have given you two a group control number with the Chinese Travel Service. A CTS representative will meet you when you arrive. You are to fly to Hong Kong on Thursday, arriving Friday morning. CTS will do your travel arrangements and have your tickets from there to Beijing and wherever else you want to go."

"Thank you," they both said.

"Thank the Vatican for sponsoring you. Otherwise it would be a long time before such a request could be processed. Also you will be supplied with an English-speaking guide and driver wherever you go. We have requested a guide named Liu Chow Lim. She is Assistant Professor of Chinese History at Sun Yat Sen University in Beijing."

"That will be very helpful," Milt thanked the man. "How do we pay for all this?"

"Since your trip is of unknown length and all of your destinations are not set, we will ask you for a deposit of $20,000. Once you exceed that, we will bill you every few days. Satisfactory?"

"Will you take a check?" Milt suggested.

"No check. Cash, please. You may bring cash back tomorrow at 10 AM."

Milt and Rid were ushered out of the offices. Once on the street, Rid said, "I wonder how much of that $20,000 will end up in his pocket?"

"He'll have to split it with whoever was watching through the mirror," Milt added. "Let's go to the Alitalia office on the Via Veneto and get our tickets for Hong Kong."

"Good idea. I hope we get this Liu Chow Lim as a guide. She should know the places Marco Polo wrote about. Perhaps she even knows about Prester John," Rid pondered.

"We need to be careful how much we reveal about the real reason for the trip," Milt admonished.

"You're right. One other thing. With all that red tape, it's unlikely any of the Defenders will be there, unless they are already in China."

"They could be. Plus, we will have to use our real names for the airline tickets. Because we have to use these passports with the visas," Milt said.

"Do you think they could monitor our travel plans?" Rid already knew the answer.

Milt spoke it. "Probably."

SEVENTEEN

China

Now that Hong Kong was part of China, Rid and Milt were subjected to a thorough search of their luggage by customs officials. They were required to make a listing of the camera, laptop computer, and other equipment they were bringing into China. Only then were Rid and Milt permitted to leave the arrival hall. They stepped out into a swarm of humanity. There were people everywhere, shouting things like "taxi!", "need guide please," hotel names, and travelers' names for those who had made arrangements in advance. The duo snaked their way through the crowd and then saw a desk at the far end of the hall, away from the throng. It had a sign on it that said CTS. They went to the desk.

"I'm Ridley Taylor and this is Milt Young. We understand you have some arrangements to get us to Beijing."

"Let me look," the Hong Kong Chinese said in his best British accent. He studied a long list of travelers.

While he was studying the list, another Chinese guide came to the desk and said his group was ready. The desk man said "Excuse me please. He has a large group." He left the desk and went outside to arrange transportation for the tourists from Japan. They were slow because they all were taking pictures. Finally, they were all on a bus and the clerk came back to the desk.

"I have found you on the list," he said. "You are group tour number 1576. Remember that as you will need to check in with us each time you change cities."

"What about getting us to Beijing?" Milt asked.

"Let me look," he answered as he again picked up his list. This time, after a short read, he opened a file drawer behind him and extracted a file. "Here are your tickets for the 6 AM flight tomorrow. It's the first available flight. Also, there is a voucher for two rooms tonight at the Shangri-La Hotel. You take a taxi there, please."

"We are supposed to have a guide assigned to us. Does your list say anything about that?"

"Let me look," came the expected reply. After more reading, he said, "Liu Chow Lim is to meet your flight in Beijing tomorrow. She will be at the CTS desk."

"Thank you," Milt said. "Do we have to check in here, tomorrow?"

"Oh no. China Air will have your clearance, and they will confirm to us that you were on the flight. This is modern China. We give our tourists great freedom."

"I'm sure," Rid said sarcastically.

The two caught a taxi, an old dark green Rolls Royce to their hotel in Kowloon. They were close to the ferry terminal to Hong Kong island. Most of the hotels, restaurants, and shops were close to them on the Kowloon Peninsula. Milt took a piece of paper from his billfold.

"Here's the name of the British MI6 contact. When I called Jeremy in London he said this Che Lo Chang could provide us with weapons. He was to call to identify me as a retired MI6 operative and you as from your former employer, the CIA."

"Let's go see him. You got the address?"

"Yes. It's in the flotilla of junks at the north end of Hong Kong. We'll find him."

They took the Star ferry over to Hong Kong across one of the most beautiful harbors in the world. Between the mountain on Hong Kong and the skyscrapers on both sides, the straight between the island and Kowloon was busy with all sorts of ships. When they left the ferry, they took a taxi to the floating village. There was a large restaurant boat covering the entrance to the flotilla.

"I'm hungry, Milt. How about you?" Rid questioned.

"Yeah. We haven't eaten since last night on the plane. Let's stop in here. Maybe we can get directions to Chang's boat."

After ordering sea slug soup and what was called chicken (but probably was something else) lo mein, the two asked the waitress if there was a directory of the junks, so they could find someone.

"Most difficult," she said. "Junks go in and out to sea every day. They tie up wherever they can when they return."

"How do you tell then which belongs to a certain person or family?" Rid asked.

"All the boats have a number on the side and back. Most also have the family name on the bow. The police publish a directory of the numbers, but we aren't allowed to have one," she answered.

"I guess we will just have to look around," Milt said as the food arrived. Even the lo mein noodles were pasty, but the Tsing Tao beer was good.

After lunch, they set out to find one boat out of the nearly 200 lashed together in a floating village. There were grocery boats, boats cooking food for sale, garbage boats, and even a clothing store going up and down the small canals between the rows of boats. After two hours of walking from boat to boat, a small Chinese boy approached Rid and Milt. "You looking for Mr. Chang?"

"Yes. Where is he?" Milt replied.

"Please to follow me," he said as he led them back the way they came.

Five boats back, the boy opened the cabin door and pointed inside. They walked in to a large cabin that served as kitchen, dining room, and bedroom for the junk's captain. A huge, blubbery man rose with some difficulty from the table.

"Which of you is Milt Young?" he questioned.

"That's me. You heard from Jeremy at MI6?"

"Yes. I have what you need at a special discount price," he said with a toothy smile.

"Aren't you with MI6 also? Won't they pay?" Milt went on.

"No. I am freelance. When the British relinquished their control over Hong Kong to the Communist government, they took all of their staff back to England. They made arrangements for me to be their agent here, but it's pay for items of information or goods on delivery."

"I see. How do you stay in contact?" Rid wanted to know.

"Let me show you." He waddled to the back wall of the cabin and removed one of the wood panels. The three of them stepped inside another room that was loaded with computers and communications equipment.

"Wow! This is quite a setup," Rid said.

"British equipped Chang before they left," the Chinaman replied.

"Very impressive," Milt said. "What about the weapons?"

"They are here," he said as he opened a cabinet on the side wall. Inside was an array of firearms from handguns to automatic rifles.

Milt found his favorite, an MI6-issued Walther PPK. Rid chose a Remington .38. They briefly discussed the need for an automatic, but decided it would be to hard to conceal as they kept traveling.

"What about airport security? Do they check for metal?" Rid said as he felt the weight of his new gun.

"No. Once you are in China and under CTS control, there are no further checks, unless you don't file and follow your plan. Since Hong Kong is now part of China, there are no security checks for flights within the country."

"Let's talk price," Milt was getting eager to leave.

"Two hundred U.S. dollars for the Walther and $150 for the Remington," he offered.

"That's robbery," Milt shouted. "And you're supposed to be one of us."

"That's why such a good price. Guns are not easy to get in China. Also, the price includes forty-eight rounds of ammunition for each piece."

"We'll give you $200 for the lot," Rid countered.

"Okay. Because we are members of the same team. Promise me though, if you are caught, you won't reveal my name."

"We have already forgotten it and where you live," Milt assured him.

They said their goodbyes and had the restaurant call them a taxi to take them back to the ferry terminal to Kowloon. Back in their hotel, they discussed what they should ask Liu Chow Lim to show them.

"I think we should start the other way around. Let's have her show us what she thinks is important about Marco Polo's visit to China. Then, if there is something specific, we can ask at the end," Rid suggested.

"Good idea. I have a feeling that Professor Lim is going to be very helpful," Milt replied.

"I hope so," Rid said as he left Milt's room. "Let's eat in the hotel tonight. They have a French restaurant here. The Margeaux, it's called."

"Maybe they'll have a bottle of their namesake wine," Milt said eagerly.

"I hope so!" Rid said for the second time.

EIGHTEEN

Beijing

When Milt and Ridley found the China Travel Service desk in the Beijing airport, there was a small, beautiful, young woman standing off to the side.

"Are you Mr. Taylor and Mr. Young?" she inquired.

"Yes," Rid said. "You must be our guide, Liu Chow Lim."

"I am Liu Chow Lim. I am honored to be your guide as you are studying my favorite person, Marco Polo," she said. "I wrote my doctoral thesis on his time in China."

"That's wonderful. You will be a great help to us," Milt said. "Can we move on now?"

"After I clear you with the CTS desk." She turned to the man behind the desk and said, "Would you please clear tour number 1576 as arriving in Beijing?"

She said it in Mandarin Chinese, but the two sleuths understood she was asking for approval of their visit to the capital city. Once outside, she led them to a white minivan. She introduced us to the driver, another Mr. Du, like the taxi driver in Hong Kong. Rid began to wonder if all drivers were called Du, or if that word meant *driver.* Of course it could just be coincidence. In any event he couldn't ask the driver, who spoke no language other than his own dialect of Mandarin. He turned out to be an excellent driver as he whizzed the van through the throng of bicycles of every description that clogged the streets.

As they were moving along, Milt nudged Rid and whispered, "Did you see the two guys in black suits watching the various cars being loaded at the airport?"

"Yeah. One of them took a good look at us and at the van. He may have written down our license number."

"It seems the Defenders of the Faith of Prester John already have a presence in China," speculated Milt.

"We'll have to be on alert and ready for anything. I hope we don't endanger Liu or our driver," Rid replied.

Liu turned from her front seat and said, "Did I hear my name?"

"Yes," Milt said. "We thought you might tell us what you have planned for us."

"I plan to give you a suggested outline when we reach your hotel. We are almost there. See ahead. The Sheraton. It has one of the largest friendship stores in the city."

The hotel was a twenty-story skyscraper soaring above the shacks that lined both sides of the street like a giant monolith. After checking in, Liu took the two travelers into a lounge. She ordered tea for all. Then she began her outline.

"I told you I wrote my doctoral thesis on Marco Polo's time in China. I wrote it in chronological order, following his notes."

"I thought his notes were back in Venice," Milt said. "I viewed microfilm of them there just last week."

"The San Georgio Basilica. Yes, I was there several years ago, preparing for my thesis. They allowed me to copy their microfilm. We will use it as our basis of study."

"That's wonderful," Rid said. 'We are fortunate to have such an expert guide. And one so beautiful, too!"

She blushed. She had raven black hair and big, dark eyes. Her skin was smooth as silk without a blemish, almost like porcelain. She was small but had a good figure. Milt made a mental note to try to keep Rid from becoming too involved with her.

"Thank you, Mr. Taylor. You make me blush."

"Please, can we use first names? I'm called Rid, and this is Milt."

"I am Liu, Mr. Taylor. Oh, excuse please, Rid and Milt."

"That's better. Now, back to your plan for us."

"In Polo's early years he followed the caravan trading routes from Europe to China. I thought we would look at just parts of it that are in China. We'll travel the well-known Silk Road to Nanking. It gives one the best feel for how his descriptions match the sites today. We'll return to Beijing to study his time at the court of Kublai Khan at the Imperial City. Finally we will briefly look at his efforts to find a mythical Christian king that, he believed, lived near here."

"I saw something about that in the notes I read in Venice," Milt seized the opportunity. "His name was Prester something and Polo believed he had been killed by Genghis Khan,"

"That's right. His name was Prester John. He claimed to have a vast empire and a vast treasure. But, I believe, Polo was wrong about Genghis Khan being his killer. They were more than a generation apart in age, with this John being the oldest," she explained. "In any event, he left directions to the palace of Prester John in the separate notes from his later years that our University Library houses. I have been to the area once, but did not find anything."

"We'll help you look this time. Maybe we will be lucky," Milt said excitedly.

"We will start tomorrow at nine and drive the caravan route to Xian. That's where Emperor Chin had himself entombed with an army of 6,000 terra cotta soldiers, in battle formation, buried in front of him."

"I've seen pictures of that. He wanted to be sure he could beat whatever enemy he might face in the afterlife. Right?" Rid asked.

"Yes, it's about a six-hour drive. We will stay over in Xian tomorrow night and return to Beijing by part of the Silk Road the next day. Also, please do not drink the water. Even in the hotel. They'll provide you each with one bottle of pure water each day. And you can buy more in the friendship store. They even have Evian there. You should now rest and unpack. I will return at seven tonight and take you to dinner at the Temple of the Moon."

She got up to leave. The two visitors walked her to Mr. Du's waiting van. As the van drove away, the two men in black suits from the airport got out of a parked car. They walked toward the lobby. Milt grabbed Rid and pulled him inside. They hid behind a magazine kiosk in the far corner of the lobby. They saw one of the men hand an envelope to the desk clerk. They watched as the clerk put the envelope in the box for room 1504, Milt's room. The men went up the elevator.

"Now is as good a time as any to confront them," Rid said.

"Agreed," answered Milt. "Let's see what's in that envelope first.

He went to the desk and retrieved the message. He pulled out a sheet of paper.

It was blank.

NINETEEN

Beijing

After picking up the phony envelope, Milt and Rid took the elevator to their rooms on the fifteenth floor. When they arrived at Milt's room, they heard muffled voices inside. They drew their weapons, silently opened the door, and jumped into the room in a crouched position. The two men dressed in black suits turned, drew their curved daggers, and took a step toward the Janus twosome. Rid shot one of them between the eyes, and he was dead before he hit the floor. The other immediately dropped his dagger. He then turned, ran out the balcony, and threw himself out into space. He splattered in the parking lot.

Rid said, "Death before dishonor. Huh?"

"I'd say. Somewhat dumb, too, if they think their dagger is faster than your bullet," Milt replied.

They called the desk, who connected them with hotel security. They were already investigating the fallen body in the lot. Milt gave them the room number. Two armed security guards were there within three minutes. One spoke Hong Kong English.

"What has happened here, please?" he asked.

"When we came to our room, there were two men here. They pulled daggers like this one," Milt said, pointing to the one on the floor. "There was a lot of confusion. The one that jumped at me pulled a gun, too. He took a shot at us, but it hit his partner. Then he turned, ran out the to the balcony and jumped."

"Where is the gun?" he wanted to know.

"He had it with him when he jumped," Rid replied.

"The police have been called. They will be here any moment. Please to sit down. Touch nothing. We will wait for them," the guard ordered.

Sitting side by side on the sofa, Milt slipped his Walther PPK into Rid's jacket pocket. As if on cue, Rid said he needed to go to the bathroom. Once there, he placed both guns in the toilet tank, high on the wall above the stool. He pulled the chain to flush the toilet to be sure it didn't stick. Then he returned to the main room as the police arrived. There was a detective, his partner, and two others dressed as soldiers with Uzi automatics.

Through the guard acting as an interpreter, Rid and Milt repeated their story. The detective put on white cloth gloves. He picked up the dagger and turned it over in his hands. He pointed at an emblem on the hilt. It was the same crest Milt had seen in Venice. The picture of the dagger in the middle of the crest. The letters D and P on the left, F and J on the right.

"You recognize this?" came the interpreted question,

"No. Never saw it before," Milt answered.

"You are to come to headquarters. Something stink like fish here. Perhaps you will be more cooperative there so we can clear up this situation," the detective said.

"May we call our guide to tell them where we are?" Rid asked. "She is supposed to pick us up at seven."

After asking the question and getting the answer, the interpreter said, "He say it is okay for you to call guide. But I must listen to conversation."

"I'll call now. She gave me her pager number," He placed the call and recorded a message. "Where are we going?" Rid wanted to include it in the message.

"Central police station on Guanghow Street," the guard relayed.

Rid called the pager again and left the address. They were taken to the station in a large, Russian-made Zil. It must have been left over from when the Russians had large numbers of technical advisors in China after the Communists came to power. When they arrived, Rid and Milt were separated and placed in separate interrogation rooms. Each was asked the same set of questions.

"Tell again the story of what happened. Where is the gun? No gun was found in the parking lot. Where is your gun?"

Both Rid and Milt were trained espionage agents by their respective CIA and MI6 teachers. Both could handle any interrogation. Each replied to the gun question, "I don't have a gun. Someone in the parking lot must have picked it up before the security guard got there."

"Do you know the two dead men?"

"No. I never saw them before."

"What is the meaning of the letters D.P.F.J?"

They each could truthfully answer, "I don't know," because the interrogator had the letters in the wrong order.

A police messenger entered the room and handed the officer in charge a note.

"It says a search of your room did not turn up any weapons. Perhaps you are accurate that someone in the parking lot found the gun."

"It must have been that way," the two answered in separate rooms almost simultaneously.

The messenger came into the room again and whispered something in the officer's ear. He said, "Excuse please. I must go out for a short time." Though Rid and Milt couldn't see, they suspected their guide, Liu, had arrived. This was confirmed by the interrogators when they came back.

"Your guide, Liu Chow Lim, has vouched for you as being here on a government permit to study and write about Chinese history. Our apologies for detaining you. You must understand we have to explore all possibilities in a matter like this."

"I understand. You were just doing your job. You were doing it well," each answered to help the policeman save a little face.

They left the station with Liu, who suggested they may as well go eat as it was almost seven. She had Mr. Du drop them off at Tiananmen Square. From there they were to walk to the restaurant. She pointed out the Imperial Palace at the top of the square and the various ministries in the government buildings along the sides of the huge square. The crowd seemed large, but, Liu explained, this was but half noon size. As they were walking across the square, an older lady in the traditional gray jacket and slacks slipped an envelope under Milt's arm, saying, "You take. You take." She disappeared.

Not wanting to return to the police station, he quickly slipped the envelope into his pocket, When they reached the restaurant, and Liu had ordered Peking duck for all, it was her turn to ask what happened.

Rid told the story again and added the line of questions the police asked. He then said, "We did not tell them that we have a suspicion as to who the men were. When Milt was in Venice, a priest at San Georgio was stabbed with a dagger like these two carried. We also think if you read the initials on the dagger's crest across, rather than down, it says D.F.P.J. Defenders of the Faith of Prester John. You mentioned him earlier as a site we might visit."

"Yes, we have a permit for three days from now," she said. "But why were these men after you?"

"They believe we are seeking Prester John's treasure," Milt explained.

"Are you after treasure? Is that your true purpose?" the guide asked warily.

"It's time for the truth. We were hired to find it by an anonymous patron. Our intent, however, is to cooperate with your government and turn any artifacts we find over to them," Rid replied.

"One last question: Did you shoot the man?"

"I did. As long as we are coming clean, we did bring weapons in case these Defenders were here. We hope you will keep our confidence and still be our guide," Rid pleaded their case.

"I want even more to be your guide, if we have a chance to confirm the actual existence of Prester John, But, please, no guns," she said.

"There may be more of these Defenders. They killed some people in Ethiopia that we were working with. We have to be prepared to keep you safe," Milt tried to convince her.

"If you are found with guns on my tour, I will go to prison for life along with you. There would be no trial."

"Because of the attack today, is there a way you can request armed guards to accompany us as we travel?" Milt suggested.

"That may be possible. I will explain the need to the CTS," she said.

Their dinner arrived. The crisp, roasted Peking duck was excellent. The rest of the food on the large lazy susan in the middle of the table was like the paste on the boat in Hong Kong. Milt remembered the envelope the lady had put under his arm. He took it out. It was addressed to Janus. He opened the envelope and removed a note on a fortune cookie slip. It read, "Noon tomorrow. Summer Palace. Peace." It was signed with the initials D.F.P.J.

TWENTY

Beijing

Liu had made special arrangements for Milt and Rid to visit the Ming tombs and the Summer Palace before leaving on their drive to Xian. When she picked them up at 9 AM, there was a military jeep type escort behind her.

"Our bodyguards," she said. "I hope you didn't bring guns."

"We left them in our checked luggage at the hotel," Milt assured her.

"Good. I will take you to see the Ming tombs first. Then we will go to the Summer Palace just before noon."

Beijing lies in high desert country. The dust blows all the time, and it can be cold at night. After fighting the thousands of bicycles on their way out of the city, they began to slowly climb in altitude. When they reached the Ming tombs, they were in a more verdant set of hills where it was cooler during the day, The tombs were remarkable. Each was set in a hillside cave with a broad avenue, lined with sculptures of animals and servants for the emperor's after-life. The treasures had been removed from the tombs. There was a small museum at the site. The major items had been taken to the national museum in Beijing.

After their walking tour, Liu and her group continued in the same direction to the Summer Palace. It sets on a large lake with extensive gardens. The emperor had a royal yacht made of stone, brightly painted, floating at a dock. It was loaded with tourists.

"That proves Archimedes was right about water displacement. That thing has got to be heavy," Rid said.

"Particularly with all those people on board," Milt added.

'Not to worry," Liu replied. "It has been floating here for a thousand years."

They went into the Summer Palace and toured the myriad rooms. They ended on the porch next to the lake. While standing there, they saw a lone man in a black suit and tie walking toward them. He had a white handkerchief in his breast pocket as a sign of peace. Rid pulled out his handkerchief as well and held it up for the man to see.

As he approached, the man said, "I am Benta Bengali, leader of the Chinese chapter of the Defenders of the Faith of Prester John."

"You already know our names. You and your murdering thugs had better leave us alone," Rid replied while looking at the military jeep, which had followed them all morning. "What do you want to tell us?"

"Do not desecrate the faith of our Prester for the sake of treasure. There is no treasure," he said.

"How do you know that?" Milt pressed him.

"Our order was founded over 500 years ago when the men from all the villages in the area of the Khyber Pass were asked to choose a faith to defend. Many of the people in our village were Christian. There also was rumored to be an ancient palace of Prester John somewhere in the mountains around the village. So our ancestors chose to defend the faith of Prester John. This oath has been handed down from father to son for generations. We only act when one of the suspected sites of his palace are being explored."

"That's all interesting. But, it tells us nothing about why you say there is no treasure."

"We have been searching for the palace of Prester John for all those 500 years, without success. We have searched in Ethiopia, Arabia, India, Pakistan, Nepal, and China. It is not anywhere," he answered.

"Well, if it's not anywhere, why do you object to our looking?" Milt scored the point.

"Our name is Defenders of the Faith, not Defenders of the Treasure. We protect all possible sites from desecration by plunderers."

"Your note said peace. What is your offer?" Rid demanded.

"We will not attack you at any of the sites as long as you do not find anything. We will be watching, and if you succeed, we will fight to preserve our sworn oath. You have weapons we learned yesterday. Are you armed now?"

"We have no weapons today. But if you are planning anything, you should know we have a military escort in that jeep in the parking lot," Milt said.

"We are honorable men, simply carrying out the sworn oath of our fathers and their fathers before them. When I came in peace today, it means no harm can come to you."

"Why are you willing to let us continue to search with your men watching?" Rid asked.

"We have studied your company, Janus International, and we know you found a 450-year-old list from Dr. Faust. You also found a treasure chest lost during the Third Crusade. We believe you bring a different set of skills to the search. We, too, would like to confirm the actual existence of Prester John. Our young people today are beginning to question the sanctity of our oath."

"Will you tell us the sites you are protecting?" Rid went on.

"Yes. As an elder, I can be the one to list them for you," Benta suggested.

Milt explained, "Our travel documents say we are in China to study the writings of Marco Polo. Our guide, Liu Chow Lim, is a professor of Chinese history. She specializes in Marco Polo's living in China. She must be kept safe."

"We will keep all of you safe unless you try to remove anything you find," he promised.

"It's almost like you want to hire us to do something we are already doing," Rid commented.

"We know you have already been paid $100,000 to fund the search. We also know your company has significant resources and you already have an employer for this search."

"Your people must have had more time in our offices than we thought," Milt mused. "Our employer asked to remain anonymous. We have speculated that he may be a man who is calling himself Johnathan Presterman. He is buying up the world's weak electric generation facilities. We sure would like to see some pictures of him. He may be our nemesis from the lost Crusade treasure affair."

"We could get rid of him for you if you like," Bengali offered.

"No. We only kill in self-defense. Your men in Rome and here pulled their daggers on us," Rid said.

"A most unfortunate loss. But now, it is better that we call a truce, rather than fight. When will you look at the site here in China?" he asked.

"In two days," Milt replied. "We are going to follow Marco Polo's path to Xian today and return to Beijing by the Silk Road tomorrow. Then we will go to the site the next day."

"I will call you at your hotel tomorrow night to confirm your visit," the Defender said.

"Just give us your number and we'll call you when we get in," Milt suggested.

"No. Our number is secret. I will keep calling until I get you. I am happy we have agreed to this truce," he said as he prepared to leave.

"Our cooperation will last as long as you do the things we have discussed. No violence."

"No violence," he repeated as he walked away.

Liu had been standing away from the conversation. As the stranger left, she walked back to Rid and Milt. "Is he connected to the two bodies from yesterday?"

"Yes. He was their boss," Rid replied.

"We should tell the authorities. We could be accused of withholding important information. Years in a dungeon could result," she said.

"He has a lot of information for us. He knows about almost all the suspected sites of Prester John's Palace, including the one here," Rid explained.

"You not like Liu Chow as your guide?" she asked sadly.

"We like Liu Chow very much. You are main guide. We will just get extra information from their studies," Rid lifted her chin as he spoke.

She smiled, "We should not have the army escort see us with him."

"He has promised us no harm will come to any of us," Milt replied.

"Then I will tell them they are no longer needed. But when we go to the site, I want to reverse myself, You two should bring your guns."

"Yes ma'am!" they said in unison.

They then drove on to Xian, arriving after dark. The next morning they toured the amazing tomb of Emperor Chin, who had himself buried in his war chariot, fronted by 6,000 life-size terra cotta soldiers. They also stopped at a prehistoric site of a family that lived in the Stone Ages. The next day, they made the long drive back to Beijing along the famous Silk Road. It was after 10 PM when they got to the hotel. As they entered Milt's room, the phone was ringing.

TWENTY-ONE

New York

The same day Young, Taylor, and Liu were travelling the Silk Road back to Beijing, Johnathan Presterman was meeting at the offices of Richards and Clark, investment bankers, in New York. Their offices were on several floors of a sixty-story skyscraper on Park Avenue. Presterman had his chief accountant and operations manager with him. His external accountants, Lagger, Brown, Zachery, Wyatt and Reeder, were also there.

The Richards team was led by a partner, Samuel Gold. He had Senior Analyst Donna Williams and two junior analysts with him. All of them specialized in electric utilities.

"We're here today to discuss two things," Presterman began. "First, we seek your opinion on the debt rating that would be assigned to any long-term bonds we may choose to issue. Second, we want you to be our primary advisors and bankers for any acquisitions we make."

"We are prepared to help you with both with one exception," Gold replied. "Where we already have a contract with one of your target utilities, we could not assist you in their acquisition."

"Understood. We would employ another banker on a case-by-case basis," Presterman replied. "Now let me be more specific. With me today are our external accountants from L. B. Z. W. and R, and my two most senior officers, Charles Becker from accounting, and William Clements, an experienced manager of electric generation plants. All of us are prepared to discuss EPIC's growth and future directions. We have prepared a file of information in the format you suggested. Here is a copy for each of you. Before we start to review the files, I have a few slides I want to show to give you a capsule of the success we have had in our first few years."

The room darkened, a screen rolled down from the ceiling at the end of the conference table and a picture came on, saying EPIC, Energy Producers International Corporation. The next slide was a line chart showing:

Year	Revenues	Net Gain
2000	$788 Mil	$124 Mil
2001	$3.8 Bil	$603 Mil
2002	$11.3 Bil	$2.0 Bil
2003 Projected	$25.0 Bil	$5.0 Bil

"The numbers, as impressive as they are, tell only part of the story. Here is why I believe we are at an excellent time to gain a huge share of the electric generation market." Another slide came on the screen as Presterman continued to speak. "We are in a buyer's market. The troubled economies in Asia, high inflation in South America, and the current recession and fear of terrorist activities in the U.S. have caused smaller utilities to seek larger partners. Second, the efficiencies gained by consolidation of companies create huge profits for the shareholders. Third, electricity can be better networked, providing power where it is needed, when it is needed. While Enron failed from alleged improper activities in their natural gas operations, their electric trading business showed the profit potential. Finally, I have proposed an alliance with other financially sound utilities."

"I saw a piece in the *Wall Street Journal* recently about the meeting you held in Paris," Gold said. "Have you had much response?"

"Yes. So far we have commitments to buy stock for 26 percent of the $15 billion we want to market. And it's only been ten days since the meeting. I'm confident we will reach our goal," Presterman said proudly.

"That's very good," Gold was impressed. "Now Johnathan, or do you prefer John, let's go to my office to discuss our arrangements with your company. We'll leave these experts to go over the numbers. My own view of your bond rating," he said for the benefit of his staff, "is that it will come down as AA+, the second highest rating. It would be AAA if you had a longer history."

"I prefer Johnathan, Samuel. I think AA+ is a fair rating. It will challenge us to work for the triple A and the lower interest cost associated with the higher rating."

"Call me Sam. Please follow me."

The two principals left the discussions and went up the winding staircase two floors to the executive floor. Gold had the southeast corner office looking across the East River to Queens and Brooklyn, and south past the Empire State Building, to Wall Street and the harbor beyond. The absence of the World Trade Center towers caused Presterman to pause looking south. "It's a sad sight, I know," said Gold. "I was here in the office on September 11 when the planes hit. The smoke and the collapse of the towers is something I will never forget. But it must now be the resolve of businesspeople like us to help rebuild our economy and world leadership position. To that end, Johnathan, I have a proposal for you to consider." Gold extracted a proposed contract from his desk drawer.

"I agree we must move forward, Sam. Let's see what you have suggested," Johnathan replied as he changed to his negotiation posture.

"Here is what we propose. A fee that is 2 percent lower than our regular agreement. We'll do the due diligence work along with your staff and accounting firm. We will also certify the acquisitions as beneficial to your shareholders. This gives you some protection from minority shareholder law suits later on."

"I'll have my lawyers and my acquisitions chief, Roy Posner, look it over. I'm sure most of it will be fine. Who knows, though, you may want to buy some of our stock to get in on the action. We could offer you some Treasury shares at a special price in return for, say, a 3 percent reduction in fees."

Gold replied, 'We must separate our investment banking and advisory business from our own holdings so we couldn't tie any fee reduction to your stock," Gold said. "I already planned, though, to pass along your story to my chief investment partner. Are you on the big board?"

"Not yet. We have applied for listing on the New York Stock Exchange. They also want a longer history. For now, we are on NASDAQ and the Brazilian exchange in Rio."

"Is there any other way I can help you?" Sam offered.

"We are currently looking for office space here in Manhattan. We need about 120,000 square feet. We plan to move our headquarters here to be close to the markets and to you."

"If you want close to us, there are three vacant floors in this building, down on 15, 16, and 17. Each has about 35,000 usable square feet."

"That may do nicely. I'm taking an apartment in the Waldorf Towers, so it would be an easy walk."

"I'm very impressed, Johnathan, with what you have accomplished in such a short time. I look forward to a long relationship," Sam said to end their meeting.

"It is only the beginning," Presterman said. "My dream will be fulfilled when EPIC controls more than half the world's power supply." He rose, turned, and strode out of the office.

TWENTY-TWO

Beijing

Milt and Rid ordered breakfast delivered to Rid's room so they could plan the visit to the suspected site of Prester John's palace.

"What do you think of this so-called peace the Defenders have offered?" Rid asked.

"I have zero confidence they will honor it. They have raped and killed the Keenes' friends, stabbed a priest, killed guards, and made two attempts on us," Milt lectured.

"I agree. We don't share anything with them. Even if we find something today we should pretend that we didn't," Rid went on. "We can always go back when they aren't looking."

"It's time to go. Liu should be downstairs," Milt said as he rose.

The two checked their weapons to make sure they were secure in their pockets. Then they took the elevator to the lobby. Liu was waiting by the front door. Mr. Du and his van were just outside.

When they got in the car, Liu turned and said, "Earlier, I saw the man from the Summer Palace talking to that bellman over by the desk. Then he left and drove away. I don't like him."

"Neither do we," Milt said. "He probably asked the bellman to let him know when we left the hotel."

"Yeah!" Rid added. "Maybe the bellhop has his phone number. Let's ask when we get back."

"Tell us more about the site we are visiting, Liu," Milt changed the subject.

"Okay. As you know, it is the site Marco Polo identified as the palace of Prester John. There has never been a major or consistent dig at the site. The earthquake of 1834 left it in rubble and covered up most of the area. A few minor digs are always in process. Mostly students from the university. It is a large area. Perhaps 100 acres. That's part of why Polo thought this could be the Prester's headquarters. There is an aquifer with ample water for such a place. Although, under our government, we are not allowed to water grass or trees. So, it is very dusty on the surface. Polo was here, staying with Kublai Khan, from 1275 to 1292. That's seventeen years he had to search. While his notes describe the site, before the earthquake, in some detail; he never found any treasure."

"Let's read his notes about the site again," Milt suggested.

They passed the pages around as they continued to drive south out of the capitol city. About thirty minutes later, Rid exclaimed, "Here's something that may be of interest. Marco is describing the mosaic floor of the main room. He says it looks like a rough map of the world as it was at the time. I'd sure like to see that."

"It has never been found," Liu answered. "Pieces of mosaic have been found, but they are pieces of borders or pictures from the walls."

"I'm with Rid," Milt interrupted, "I'd sure like to see that map."

"I can locate the spot of the main hall for you," Liu went on. "But don't be too disappointed when you don't find the map."

"It seems to me that Marco Polo would have made a drawing of the map?" Rid queried. "He was always careful about such things."

"My thesis discussed that possibility. One of Polo's journals never was found. We surmised it must have been the one with the map. He regularly sent his journals back to Venice. It probably was lost along the way."

"Or, thinking it had something to do with Prester John's treasure, he hid it at Kublai Khan's court in the Forbidden City," Milt mused.

"I have seen the Polo materials from there. They are at the National Museum. The missing journal is not there. We can go look, if you like."

"We like," both said in unison.

As they pulled into the parking area of the site, they saw Bengali standing by the entrance. He smiled and nodded to them as they entered, gestures that were not returned.

TWENTY-THREE

Beijing

Rid, Milt, and Liu spent the next three hours wandering around the site. There was not a lot to see. A few places had been excavated. They examined each of them carefully. The one of most interest was a new hole dug in the corner of what must have been the great hall. The hole was about ten feet deep and six feet across. There was a homemade ladder to the bottom. Rid climbed down to get a closer view of the floor. There were a few mosaic tiles, but not enough to determine if it was a map or some simple design. He did imagine the outline of small fish, no doubt the picture that excited Marco Polo and drew him to conclude this was the palace of Prester John. Rid climbed back up the ladder.

Shaking his head, he said, "Nothing of interest down there."

Benta Bengali had followed the group around the site. He smiled at Ridley's proclamation. As the three walked past him on the way to the exit, he stated, "I knew you would find nothing here."

Milt cut him short, saying, "If you really are trying to preserve the faith of this Prester John, you should be raising money to finance a proper dig of this site."

"We have, but the Chinese government won't allow anyone but their own people to dig," the Defender answered.

"You can stop following us now. We will be leaving China in a few days," Rid barked.

"We will know when you go. We will also be at the other suspected sites to observe your actions," Bengali countered.

"Be on guard then. I don't like threats!" Milt replied as they reached the entrance.

Once in the car, Rid told the others, "When I said nothing down there, that was for his benefit."

"I assumed as much," Milt interrupted.

"What did you find?" Liu asked, with excitement in her voice.

"The floor definitely was mosaic. I could make out the rough outline of an early Christian fish. More important, I think there was a part of the arc of another one that was mostly still covered with dirt," Rid explained.

"Why is that important?" Milt questioned.

"What if the floor was a map, with seventy-two fish displayed?" Rid let the two of them answer.

"Prester John claimed to have seventy-two kings under him," Liu offered.

"Right," Milt added, "The floor could well be a map of his entire domain."

"It also would prove this was at least one of the places where our friend P.J. lived. I sure wish we could find Polo's missing journal. He must have made a copy of the map," Ridley lamented.

"There is one other possibility," Liu said.

"What's that?" Milt wanted to know.

"In the materials at our University Library, where I studied for my thesis, there were several large, rolled-up pieces of tanned oxen hides. They were mostly pictures of scenes from Kublai Khan's court. I was not permitted to unroll them all."

"Can we see them?" Rid asked,

"Yes. I can get permission for a visit. It may take a day or two," the guide replied.

"Hopefully, we will be able to keep that visit a secret from our Indian monitor," Rid said. "I want to talk to that bellhop when we get back to the hotel."

"I can plan a ditch for when we go. The friendship store in the hotel has a rear exit," Milt suggested.

"Better than that is the way we do it in China," Liu explained. "You know traffic is terrible here. Like this broad boulevard we are on now. What if I had a second car along the inside of the street going the other way. We could simply stop, walk to the other car, and go the other way. It's 200 yards to the next turn around. In this traffic it would take them at least five minutes."

"Sounds good," Milt liked the plan.

"What would you like to do until I get permission?" Liu queried.

"I'd like to see the Great Wall, so I can visualize the obstacle that Genghis Khan faced," Milt explained.

"Me, too," Rid chimed in.

"I'll set that up for tomorrow," Liu said as they pulled up to the Sheraton. "You're on your own for dinner tonight."

"We'll probably eat here," Rid said. "You have a big date tonight?"

"Yes. We are going to the all China gymnastics finals at the stadium."

"Sounds exciting," Rid said without much conviction.

When the two entered the hotel they spotted the bellman Bengali had hired.

His name tag said Tommy Huong. When they got to Rid's room, they ordered drinks and ice from room service. They asked specifically for Huong to deliver the order. A few minutes later, the phone rang.

"Excuse please. Tommy Huong not bring drinks. He was hit by car in parking lot a few moments ago. Hit and run. Huong dead."

"Okay. Send anyone. And double that drink order," Rid answered. "Huong is dead. Hit-and-run victim," he said to Milt as he hung up the phone.

"They don't leave loose ends, do they?" Milt replied.

"Let's just make sure we aren't a loose end."

TWENTY-FOUR

China

When Liu Chow Lim picked up the two sleuths the next morning to take them out to the Great Wall, she said, "I have good news. We have an appointment at the University Library tomorrow. The head of the Archives Department, Dr. Wu Ling, remembers me and said he would meet with us himself."

"Does he know who we are and what we are hoping to find?" Rid asked.

"He knows I am conducting a research trip on Marco Polo and his writings about Prester John," she replied.

"Will we have free access to the drawings?" Milt interjected.

"Probably not. The oxen skins they are on are very brittle. I'm sure Dr. Ling will want to oversee our use of any drawings."

"How many of them are there?" Milt went on.

"As I remember, there are around thirty drawings. Polo kept almost all his notes in his journals. These skins were used only when he wanted more detail in a larger drawing."

Rid added, "We are most fortunate to have you as our guide, Liu. I feel that we may find something important."

"Let us hope so," she said. 'But now we are out of the city heading north toward the closest point of the Great Wall. As you probably know it was built around 1100 and it stretches across China's northern border from the Pacific Ocean to the Ural Mountains at our western frontier. It is over 2,000 kilometers long. The wall is some twelve meters high."

Rid interrupted, "That's almost forty feet."

"Yes, and there are watch towers every 500 meters. A little less than half a mile apart."

Rid and Milt spent the rest of the ride to the wall rereading their notes about Genghis Khan. As they arrived at the tourist visitation area, Milt joked, "Look how tall that sucker is, Rid."

"Yeah, and wide, too!" Rid shot back.

"That Genghis Khan must have been some kind of smart general to have breached this thing," Milt finished.

"It looks like there are gates about every tenth watch tower, or about five miles apart. If he could control about a thirty-mile front, he could move a lot of warriors through six gates," Rid went on. "It must have been a staggering blow to the Chinese army."

The three of them toured the wall, walking on top of it a mile or more in each direction.

"Where did the Khan cross?" Rid asked Liu.

"It is believed it was only about 100 kilometers west of here. That part of the wall is in ruins now, and no visitors are permitted," she explained.

"That's okay, we got a good feel for his battle strategy from this portion," Milt said.

After lunch at a small roadside restaurant, where nothing was fit to eat except the local unpasteurized beer and some year-old Planter's dry roasted peanuts, the group headed back to Beijing. As they traveled they made plans for the next day's visit to the University Library.

"We really must keep this a secret from our nemesis, the Defenders. I wonder if they know about the drawings?" Milt said all of a sudden.

"I have not heard of any problems at the library," Liu began. "As a teacher at the university, I would have heard if there was a break-in, or anything like that."

"Hopefully they are not aware of the drawings," Rid said.

"You know," Milt inserted, "I don't remember seeing any of the black-clad Defenders at all today. Do you think they have backed off?"

"I'd bet against that. Perhaps, when we headed north they decided not to follow," Rid suggested.

The driver, Mr. Du, said something to Liu in Chinese. She interpreted. "Du says he heard you say 'Defenders,' and he knew we are worried about them. He says 'One of the doorman at the hotel asked him casually where he was taking us today.' He told them the Great Wall."

"So maybe, they aren't interested in the Genghis Khan/Prester John connection," Milt calculated.

"I hope the doorman lived through the day," Rid said.

"Oh my," Liu said, "You two are my most dangerous and interesting clients."

"Not by our choice," Milt emphasized.

As they pulled up to the Sheraton, there were several police cars in the parking lot. When they disembarked their van, the hotel's security chief was there waiting for them.

"Where have you been today?" he wanted to know.

Liu stepped between him and the other two. "I took them to see the Great Wall today. They have been with me all day."

"I see. Another employee, a door man, was the second hit-and-run victim in as many days. This time, though the car involved was going too fast, and it crashed into that truck over there. The driver was killed. But he was wearing a black suit like the two from your room. The police will want to question you. Wait here. I will get them."

While he was gone, Rid and Milt secreted their guns under the seat of the van. In a few minutes, a detective they hadn't seen before was escorted to them. Again the hotel security chief acted as interpreter for the detective, and Liu served the same role for the twosome.

"He says his name is Foo Chen. He is assigned to traffic accident investigations. He asks what you know about these two hit-and-runs?" the security man repeated.

"Tell him we know nothing, Liu," both Rid and Milt said.

She replied to the detective and the security chief did as well.

Through the interpreters, the conversation went on.

"Who were men killed in your room?"

"We didn't know them. They were robbing our room."

"Today's death caused by someone is same black suit and carrying same curved dagger. There must be a connection."

"Liu," Rid summarized, "explain to him that after our meeting with the other detective, we have seen several of these men. We even spoke to one at the Summer Palace two days ago. They say they are the Defender's of the Faith of Prester John, a legendary Christian king who may have lived near here. They seem be to following us to keep us from doing our research on Marco Polo. Then add any details you want about our study of Polo."

She talked for some time with the Detective. He asked a few questions, which she apparently answered to his satisfaction. Finally he said something to her while nodding to the twosome. She then said, "You are free to go. I explained you have government approval for your work."

"Thank you!" Rid said while extending his hand to the Detective.

"Shu Shu," the Detective replied, first shaking their hands, then bowing as he backed away. Then he turned and went toward his car.

"Tomorrow will be another challenge," Milt said. "Do you think our plan to ditch these followers will work, Liu?"

"It will. Mr. Du is very capable driver."

"I need to get something from the van," Rid said. He returned in a moment with their weapons in his coat pockets.

When they went to the desk to get their room keys, there was a message in Rid's box. It read, "Hope you enjoyed your trip to the Great Wall, and your lunch at the roadside restaurant in Ma Ring." It was signed Bengali.

"How did he know that? Where we ate?" Milt asked.

"They must have more watchers than we think," Rid responded.

"If they kill them all, we're going to be responsible for the most deaths in China since Genghis Khan," Milt quipped.

"Perhaps" Rid smiled. "Perhaps."

TWENTY-FIVE

Beijing

The next morning it was raining and foggy in the Chinese capital city. Liu and Mr. Du were at the front door of the hotel when Rid and Milt came downstairs. As they approached the van, they saw Bengali and two other black suits get into a car in the lot.

"The fog should help us with the ditch," Milt said.

"Yeah. Maybe they'll think they lost us because of the weather. Can Mr. Du get far enough ahead of them so they won't see us leave the van?" Rid asked the guide.

" I will have him try," Liu replied as she gave instructions to the driver. He pulled into the public bus lane, where only buses and government cars were allowed. It was much faster because there were no bicycles. Unfortunately, their followers pulled into the same lane and stayed about 100 yards behind. Then, at a light, Mr. Du made it through just as it turned red. The policewoman at the corner made the pursuers stop. Another two blocks ahead, Liu said, "Now!" The van slowed and the three of them jumped from it and crossed the dirt-filled boulevard to a waiting car. As they closed the door, they saw the Defenders' car racing past the other way.

"Hooray! It worked," Rid chortled. "Let's get on to the university."

"This is your new driver, Mr. Du," Liu said with a smile.

"You're teasing me. All drivers aren't named Du," Milt challenged.

"This one is. He is the brother of your regular driver. He also drives for the CTS," she answered.

When they arrived at the Sun Yat Sen University Library, Liu led them to the rare books archives.

"This is an old friend who helped me with my thesis," she began, "He is Dr. Wu Ling, one of the world's leading experts on Marco Polo and his time in China. Dr. Ling, this is Ridley Taylor and Milt Young. They are doing research to see if there is any connection between Polo and the Christian King Prester John."

"Welcome," he said in an American accent. "Liu was one of my best students."

"Where did you pick up your accent?" Rid wanted to know.

"I got both my undergraduate and master's in Library Science at the University of Illinois. They have the world's largest university library."

"On occasion," Rid added, "they are pretty good in football and basketball, too."

"I attended one football game. Not as graceful as gymnastics," he said. "In any event, Liu says you want to see the oversize drawings of Marco Polo. I have taken them out of the vault. They are on the large table over there. Please do not touch them. I will unroll them for you when you ask. Any particular thing you are looking for."

"We won't touch. We want to see any drawings of the palace Polo thought might be Prester John's Court. Particularly one of the main hall with its mosaic floor," Milt said.

"Those would be the ones over here," the Librarian said as he began to unroll one of the hides.

"These look like scenes from a king's court," Rid commented about the first four drawings.

"Some are part of Polo's description of the Court of Kublai Khan," the Professor explained. "Others may be from the site suspected to be that of the Christian king."

Drawing number seven was lucky. It was a partial picture of what could be the mosaic floor map. By Marco Polo's time, it had already been defaced a great deal. A few sections looked like map parts of Asia and the Middle East. There was also a piece at the far left that showed what could be the Red Sea and Ethiopia. On the parts that were more complete, there were several fish symbols.

"Look at the fish," Rid said excitedly.

"Do you see," Milt added, "That three of the fish are larger than the others. And they look like they have jewels inlaid in the tiles. This one could be the site near here, this one in Ethiopia, and one in what appears to be Russia."

"It could be Samarkand, where Genghis Khan's aide suggested the Prester moved," Rid suggested. "I'd say we need to go there."

"I agree. Professor, may we take a picture of this drawing?" Milt asked.

"No flash, please," Dr. Ling cautioned.

"Okay," Milt agreed as he took out a small camera and snapped several pictures of the drawing.

"This has been most helpful, Professor Ling. Thank you very much," Rid expressed their thanks.

"You are welcome. What is your assessment of this document?" Ling queried.

"We think it may be proof that Prester John really did exist and that he moved his court around the seventy-two kingdoms he claimed to control," Milt replied.

"Then it is a most important discovery," the Professor said. "Perhaps this will help me get government funds for a more extensive dig at our site."

"Please try," Liu said. "I would love to work with you on such an important project."

After further farewells, the trio went back to the library entrance. As they were approaching the door they saw two of the three Defenders from the morning coming up the steps. They hid behind a large column as they passed and went on to the information desk. It appeared that they were unsure of what they were looking for, as after the clerk shrugged and shook her head, they backed away. Bengali gave the other one instructions and they set off in different directions.

"I hope they don't know about the Professor," Liu said.

"If they knew, they would have both gone straight there. They are looking for us," Rid tried to soothe her.

"How did they find out we came here?" Milt began. "Do you suppose they caught up to our first Mr. Du?"

"He did know we were coming here," Liu said. "I hope he is all right."

"We do, too!" Rid echoed. "If not, we have a score to settle with these Defenders."

"I suspect we'll have an opportunity to do that this evening," Milt offered. "Now, let's get out of here."

They scrambled down the side of the steps to the lot. Their second van was there.

"It looks like they didn't see this van earlier. Hop in," Rid yelled.

Once in the van, the driver turned. It was not the second Mr. Du. It was the third black suit. Only this one was not wielding a dagger. He had a gun.

TWENTY-SIX

Beijing

A short while later, Bengali and his other henchman came out to the van.

"I see you have met my other aide," he said with a smile.

Rid interrupted, "What have you done with our two drivers, you son of a bitch? You agreed to no violence."

"And you were to let us know where you were going. Manu, keep your gun on them while we search them."

They did a thorough body search of the two detectives and their guide. They took everything, including their guns, ammunition, and the camera with the pictures of Marco Polo's map. They blindfolded the three. Then one left to drive their car and the van proceeded for about half an hour to a place that still sounded like it was in the city. They were hustled from the van into a dark place down five steps to a cold room. When the blindfolds were removed they discovered they were in a Chinese version of a root cellar.

"We will develop this film," Bengali said. "Then we will talk."

"Again, you swine, what has happened to our drivers?" Milt screamed.

"They needed persuasion to tell us where to find you. They have gone to meet their ancestors," he said as he turned and left. The others followed him outside. A large metal door was lowered over the opening and they heard a bolt slide shut followed by the click of a lock. It was pitch dark in the damp enclosure. The room was eight feet by twelve feet. It was perhaps seven feet high in the middle, built like a Quonset hut arching to the floor. There were shelves along the walls but they were bare. And it was cold.

"Take my jacket, Liu," Rid offered. They both felt their way to the exchange.

"We need to figure a way out of here," Milt began. "Perhaps we can dig our way to the surface of the ground above."

"Unlikely, Milt. There is probably some cement reinforcement to keep this from collapsing."

"That's right," said Liu. "There are many of these storage places in Beijing. There is a reinforcing roof to keep it from falling during the rainy season."

"Okay. So digging is out. What else is there?" Milt went on.

"Only the door," she said. "And it's locked from the outside."

"I guess we'll just have to wait till they open the door. Let's set a plan for then," Rid suggested. "How long, Liu, will it take them to get the film developed?"

"Unless they can do it themselves, we do not have good developing services. The one-hour stores are unreliable. So it will take a while."

"Then we will wait," Rid closed. And they waited in the cold dark place for what turned out to be two days. No one brought food or water. The cold and dampness became almost unbearable. The three prisoners alternated between huddling together in the center of the room, away from the coldness of the walls, and jogging in place to increase their body heat and keep their muscles toned.

On the third morning, they could hear movement outside and the clanging of the lock. They had placed some of the bare shelves on each side of the door. Milt and Rid quickly jumped to the top shelf of each and Liu retreated to the far wall and laid on the floor. The bolt slid and the door slowly opened.

Only one of the thugs, carrying Milt's Walther PPK started to enter. He stopped when he saw Liu and began looking for the others.

At that moment, both Rid and Milt swung from their perches into the doorway. They caught the guard full in the chest with their feet. He dropped the gun as he fell back gasping. Milt rolled over him and grabbed his gun. Rid jumped on the guard and snapped his neck. He was dead before his next breath.

The noise of the scuffle caused Bengali and his other thug to run out of the adobe hut that sat next to the root cellar. Both had revolvers in their hands. Milt quickly dispatched the thug with a shot between his eyes. He then turned to Bengali, but the PPK wouldn't fire.

Bengali was saying, "Now you die for your desecration of our King Prester John." He took careful aim at Milt and was about to shoot, when a curved dagger came flying into his throat,

"What the hell?" Milt looked around.

"I found it on the guard," Rid grinned. "Pretty good toss, huh?"

"I'll say. Now let's see if there are any more of these guys around," Milt said.

Liu came out of the cellar and was pleased to see her two clients alive. She went over to the dead Bengali and began kicking his body, yelling, "For Mr. Du. For Mr. Du."

"We need to get out of here before the police are called," Rid urged.

"No one calls the police here. They fear police," Liu answered. "Besides, they have no phones."

A search of the house turned up their other belongings, the camera, and two sets of oversized prints of the pictures of the map from Prester John's palace. They then walked about two miles through a warren of mud huts. Liu kept them going until they came to a paved road. There she flagged down a truck, who took them back near their hotel. It was just before noon. As they approached the hotel they saw two policemen near the door.

"We need to go somewhere else," Rid said.

"Wait here," Liu said "I will get a taxi from the Hyatt across the street. We can go to my place."

A few minutes later she pulled around the corner and the taxi took them to her apartment, which was near the University. Once inside they discussed their next moves.

"We need to get out of town," Rid said. "Will the police be watching for us at the airport?"

"Probably. Tomorrow, I will drive you to Nanking. There you can take a train to Guilin, and from there cross into North Vietnam. That border is not so closely guarded."

"What about you?" Milt wanted to know. "Won't the police be after you?"

"Perhaps. I will explain that I had been kidnapped by those bad men, that you two rescued me, killed them in a shootout, and then fled. I don't know where you are, I will tell them."

"It might work," Rid said. "What about our guns and pictures? We can't be caught with them."

"Dispose of the guns in the river that flows through the park across the street tonight. I can send the pictures to you where ever you say."

"How?" they both asked.

"I will ask Professor Wu to include them in a diplomatic pouch. He frequently ships artifacts that way."

"Good. Have him send them to Monsignor Ricardo Corso. He is the Curator of the Vatican museum in Rome." Milt instructed.

"He probably sends things there now. Now let me see if I can find something to eat. And we all need to rest after days in that cold cellar."

After rice and noodles, washed down with plum wine, Liu took the bed, Milt the couch, and Rid the recliner. As they were about to fall asleep, Liu said, "You have been my most exciting tour, I wish a safe journey for you both."

"Thank you, Liu. We are sorry if we have put you in any danger," Rid replied. "Hopefully there are no more Defenders of the Faith in China."

"And, hopefully, Bengali did not contact his superiors, wherever they are," Milt left that thought in all their minds.

TWENTY-SEVEN

Moscow

It was 7 PM in Moscow when Roy Posner dialed EPIC's new offices in New York. He ask for his Chief Executive, Johnathan Presterman. Presterman came on the line. He started, "You have news for me, Roy?"

"Yes sir! Good news. I met today for four hours with the Energy Commissars of all the remaining states in the new Russian Federation. With the exception of the Ukraine, they all expressed interest in our offer to privatize their utilities."

"That is good news. Any talk of price?" Presterman asked.

"I told them we would want our investment bankers to review their operations and make an appraisal for each unit before we set a price. I did say we were getting other energy companies world wide to invest and that we planned to raise $15 billion in new capital. They asked if they could receive shares instead of cash. I said probably not," Roy explained.

Presterman countered, "Their economies are cash short right now. I'll bet their leaders will want the money. I don't, however, want their desire for stock to kill the deal. Tell them we will consider issuing nondividend, nonvoting, Class B stock as an incentive for their future performance, if their governments will slow the phase-out of all subsidies and do it over a three-year period. Then, if they are in a profit position, we will convert the stock to regular shares for their prorated portion of the 49 percent held by others."

"Good idea, Johnathan. What do you want me to do about the Ukraine?"

"I don't think it will be a problem at the end of the day. Since the accident at their nuclear plant in Chernobyl, they have been buying most of their power from Belarus and the other republics. Once we have the others, we can dictate the terms of their purchase," Presterman suggested.

"Brilliant! What do you want me to do next?" Posner asked.

"Contact each of the Commissars individually and tell them of our willingness to consider stock as I outlined. They probably each want to know what is in the deal for them personally. Tell them we will pay an appropriate finder's fee. Also, set a time for the investment banker team to come to Russia. Make it about two weeks from now to give their governments time to debate the offer. By then Richards will have a checklist of everything they want to see."

"What about me? Should I come to New York, Johnathan?"

"No. You stay there and keep the Commissars interested. Entertain them. There must be parties in Russia with vodka and women. Make them happy."

"Yes sir. Anything else?"

"No. Goodbye."

With that phone call, the future of electricity generation in the Russian Federation was set on a new course. One more step in Johnathan Presterman's plan to control the world's power supply. "The world will still be mine," the former Sir Dean Floyd thought to himself.

TWENTY-EIGHT

Beijing

The next morning, in Beijing, Liu Chow Lim had found peasant clothes for Ridley and Milt. As they dressed, she said, "Soon two friends of mine, members of our student resistance group, will bring you train passes and travel permits. You should be able to get to the border with them. That is as much as I can do. "

"It's more than enough, We owe you a great deal and we will find a way to help you with your search for the Presbyter," Milt replied.

"In fact, we are carrying several thousand American dollars. I suspect if we were caught with it, the game would be up," Rid added.

They gave her $8,000 of the $15,000 they had between them.

"I don't want your money. I helped you because I feel you will do the right thing for China should you find the treasure of Prester John."

"We will do that if it is found. Keep the money. You can use it to help fund your dig at the site with the mosaic map," counseled Milt.

At that moment there was a knock at the door. The three were very cautious in looking outside first to make sure it was neither the police or more of the Defenders of the Faith. It was two young women.

"It is Bee Hig Lee and Lee Cor Soo, my student friends, Let them in."

Rid opened the door and the young students came in. After introductions, the one named Cor Soo said, "These papers are not the best, but they are all we could get on short notice."

She spoke in broken English and Liu helped interpret.

"We appreciate having any at all. Where did they come from and what do we owe you?"

Liu passed it along. Hig Lee said, "These are papers we have collected since our failure at Tiananmen Square. Most student groups are ready to demonstrate again, and we will need such papers if we have to evade the authorities. Liu told me you were too old to pass for students, and these are from two older people now dead. You must be careful not to let anyone get a good look at you."

"We'll be invisible," Rid chuckled. They gave the students $2,000 for their student organization. They were astonished at so much American money. Once they left, Liu Chow took the two to her car and they started along the way to Nanking. As they were traveling out of Beijing, she stopped for gas. The two fugitives stayed in the car. When Liu came out of the station, she said, "Sad news. The police have found the bodies and they are searching for the two of you."

They looked at their pictures in the Chinese newspaper she handed them. Pictures that were taken when they were in the police station just three days before.

"Perhaps we should turn ourselves in," Rid suggested. "That way you should have no problems with the law."

"Yes, we could use diplomatic means to leave China." Milt added.

"That's the answer!" Rid said excitedly. "Turn around, Liu, and take us to the American embassy. They will get us out of the country."

She dropped them off about three blocks from the embassy. They waited until she was out of sight, then they bowed their bodies and shuffled along the walk toward the U.S. compound. They were surprised their were no Chinese police at the gate. As they approached the Marine standing guard, Rid said, "I'm CIA. Code R440-1. Take us in."

The rescue code was instantly recognized. The Marine swung open the gate and the two were back on U.S. soil. As they walked toward the door of the embassy, they spied two plainclothes officers get out of a parked car across the street.

"It looks like they have been watching for us. I wonder why they didn't try to stop us," Rid asked.

"Maybe they are pleased that we eliminated the Defenders for them," Milt replied. "Could be. Anyway, I think it's time we bring our governments into the case. If this search really is tied to this Johnathan Presterman and his control of power producers, they need an early alert. I say we come clean to the CIA Station Chief and have him relay messages to Bryan Robert in Washington and Jeremy at MI6."

"Good idea. I know they'll be interested in our suspicion that Presterman is really Dean Floyd, who is wanted for treason in England," Milt agreed.

They met for about two hours with Bob Bell. A former decorated Marine, he was the manager of transportation for the embassy, which was a good cover for his leadership role of the CIA in China. He was fascinated by the story of Prester John's treasure and the tie-in to the earlier attempt at world domination through the privatization of the world's military. He remembered some of the details of the earlier scheme as he had been on a taskforce to help decide how the agency's mission might change if the plan was successful. When they finished, Bell called the Ambassador, Bill Yager, and set up an immediate meeting. After briefing the Ambassador, they went to the communications room. They sent encrypted messages to London and Washington, suggesting they all meet to establish a course of action. Two hours later, instructions came back saying a meeting had been set for the day after tomorrow at MI6's office in London. Bryan Robert would come over from Washington.

"Now we need to get to London," Rid looked quizzically at Bell.

"Not a problem," he said. "Our courier plane is scheduled to leave tomorrow morning for Washington. It frequently drops off passengers and diplomatic mail in London."

"We'll need clothes," Rid said.

"We have a supply," Bell answered. "Let me show you to your room, where you can rest and change. Please use the embassy's cafeteria for your meals and be ready to leave the compound at 6 AM tomorrow. I am pleased you chose to come in from the cold. I had been following the stories of all the killings recently here in Beijing. And I knew we didn't have any special operations going on. So I was puzzled."

"We have been involved, Bob, and I can tell you we were puzzled for a long time, too," Rid responded. "There seemed to be no end to these so-called Defenders of Prester John's faith."

Milt suggested as they were parting, "Once our governments understand the situation fully, I would guess the days of both the Defenders of Prester John and that of Johnathan Presterman will become numbered."

TWENTY-NINE

Beijing and London

The embassy limousine left the compound at precisely 6 AM with Taylor and Young, along with Ambassador Yager and CIA Station Chief Bell. A Chinese police motorcade pulled in front and back of the embassy stretch Lincoln. There was a Marine Sergeant driving and a Marine Lieutenant in the front.

"Will they try to stop us?" Rid asked.

"No," said the Ambassador. "When I am in the car it is standard procedure for them to provide an escort. My office called them last night to inform them I was going to London on today's flight. Actually, I ask permission from Secretary of State Watson. He asked me to monitor your meetings with Bryan Robert."

"Thank you for coming with us. I feel better about our chances of actually getting out of China," Milt expressed his feelings.

The trip to the airport was easy. Even though it was early in the morning, there were thousands of bicycles of every description clogging the roads. Some had rickshaw seats on the front, others had truck-like beds on the back. They were used for all types of commercial vehicles. The motorcade, however, sped through the government lane in the middle. They arrived at the airport shortly before seven and were driven to a private hangar on the far side from the terminal. As soon as they boarded the plane, they taxied out and were given clearance for immediate take-off.

Ambassador Yager and Milt tried to get a little sleep. Bob Bell asked Rid to look over the notes on the case he had made the day before. "I sent a copy of this to Bryan Robert through our secure scanner," he said.

"Good," Rid replied. "I worked for Bryan for some time, so I'm glad he personally is on the case. We need you to stay up to date in case there is any more to be done in China. Milt and I would probably not be welcomed back."

"You're right about that. They let you leave because you cleaned out a bad lot. But they won't have the welcome mat out."

"I'm worried about our guide, Liu Chow Lim. She may be called in for questioning," said Rid. "She does know part of our story about the treasure of Prester John."

"When I return to the embassy, I will ask to have her left alone. The police here would be more interested in using her as bait for you or the other group."

"It's important for you to know that she helped us because we assured her that if we did find any treasure or artifacts, that they would remain the property of the Chinese government."

"That will help with the police, if necessary," Bell replied.

The rest of the way to London, they all rested. They landed at the air base north of London where another limo waited. Bob Bell installed the other three in the car. Then he said, "I'm going back on the return flight. I think it's more important for your guide and for the operation for me to be there."

"Thank you!" Rid said as the limo pulled away.

The car dropped Taylor and Young off at Dukes, their favorite hotel near Green Park, Buckingham Palace, and the offices of MI6. It was only 9 AM London time, but the hotel had rooms for them.

"A Mister Jeremy called last night to have rooms held," the desk clerk said. "He also left you these messages."

The two of them went to Rid's room and opened the two message envelopes. The first was a message from Jeremy saying they would meet with M, Evelyn Downs, at 2 PM that afternoon. The second was from Bryan Robert saying, "I'll arrive at 10:30 and will come to Dukes. Set up an early lunch and we can discuss your findings. I want to be thoroughly briefed before the big meeting."

"Sounds like we have established some interest in our current case," Milt quipped.

"Very funny, Milt. I caught the pun. Current. Very electric. Let's get ready for the meetings."

THIRTY

London

At two o'clock that afternoon everyone except M was seated around the conference table in her private conference room. Ambassador Yager from China and CIA Deputy Director Bryan Robert from Washington represented the American government. Jeremy Househam, Assistant Chief of MI6, was there for Britain. As Big Ben struck two about a block up the Thames, the door to M's office opened and she walked in.

"Please keep your seats gentlemen. I believe I have met everyone here before, with the exception of Ambassador Yager. Welcome," she said as she took her seat at the head of the table.

"Thank you. Please call me Bill," the Ambassador started to say.

"And call me Evelyn, Evelyn Downs. I just can't get these field operatives to say anything but M.

"A pleasure M. . . I mean Evelyn," Yager quipped.

"Bryan, nice to see you again. It hasn't been too long."

"Just three years. We helped these two foil the scheme of Sir Dean Floyd to take over the world's militaries."

"Right. Ridley and Milt, I understand you think that Floyd has resurfaced."

"We sure do, M. We think he is posing as Johnathan Presterman, CEO of EPIC. It's an international cartel of energy producers. They are on an acquisition binge across the globe," Milt began.

"Let us tell you the whole story and the reasons we believe it's Floyd," Rid interrupted.

For the next half hour, Taylor and Young alternately told the story of their hiring by an anonymous benefactor to find the lost treasure of an ancient Christian king, Prester John. They covered their run-ins with the Defenders of the Faith of Prester John. They told about the pictures of the old mosaic world map from Marco Polo's search.

"Where are these pictures now?" she asked.

"Our guide in China was to mail them in a diplomatic bag to Monsignor Ricardo Corso, Curator of the Vatican Museum," Milt replied. "We aren't certain if she has done that yet."

"Might I suggest," Ambassador Yager broke in, "that we have Bob Bell go see her. He should be back in Beijing very soon. If she hasn't mailed them, he can fax them on our secure line."

Rid said, "That would be great, Ambassador. I had asked Bell to protect her."

Evelyn directed, "Call him now. Use the red phone on that side table. It is tied into our U.S./U.K. scrambled network."

While the Ambassador was calling, Bryan Robert posed a new question. "Suppose you are correct that this Presterman really is Dean Floyd and that he has another scheme for world domination. What do we do?"

Jeremy suggested, "Her Majesty's government has an arrest warrant out for him. If he is in New York as Rid says, we could simply have him arrested and extradited to England for trial."

"We'll come to that sometime soon," M interjected. "First, though, we must make certain it is Floyd. There are, as I understand it, a number of legitimate, large, privately owned utilities who have invested in his company."

"That's right," Milt added. "Their current activities with EPIC are all legal and above board. If we were to arrest him now, and it wasn't Floyd, there would be a number of lawsuits."

"I agree," Evelyn followed. "There would be any number of solicitors who would like to tap the coffers of our two governments."

"So, I repeat my question," Bryan said. "What do we do about Dean Floyd, a.k.a. Presterman?"

Ambassador Yager returned to the table and everyone looked up at him.

"I talked to Bell. He is ahead of us. He had called your guide when he returned to the embassy. He told them of your successful escape from China and of your desire to keep her safe. She still had the photographs. Bell sent a car to pick her up and we should have the pictures tonight."

"That's great!" Rid said,

"I have a suggested course of action," Milt offered.

"Let's hear it," M said.

"I think it's time for Rid and I to meet our anonymous backer. We could tell him we have some very promising pictures to show him," Milt went on.

"He won't meet face to face with you." Jeremy cautioned. "You know him by sight."

"We can cover that. We'll tell him up front that we know who he is, and that we want to join his team," Rid fleshed out the plan.

"That worked in our Lost Crusade operation," Milt added.

"Yes, but once bitten, twice shy," Bryan countered.

"He'll meet with us. There is too much at stake," Rid concluded.

"If he doesn't, that will be even more evidence that he is Floyd," Evelyn began to summarize. "Let's try this. When the pictures come, Jeremy, call us together again tonight and we will finalize the plan. Thank you each for coming."

"Before you leave, M, I plan to inform my agency and the President about what we believe is going on with EPIC," Bryan stated.

"I assumed you would. I'm on my way now to report to the Prime Minister," she said as she left the room.

The faxed pictures arrived before seven that evening, Jeremy called Ambassador Yager at the U.S. embassy, and he reached his boss, Evelyn, at her private apartment within the MI6 complex. He found Bryan, Rid, and Milt in the bar at Dukes. All of them were back in the conference room at 7:30. The pictures were passed around.

"Not much detail, is there?" Evelyn spoke first.

"You have to know the history," Milt explained. He told the story of the letter Prester John had sent to Emperor Manuel I of Byzantium, describing his seventy-two kingdoms and his vast treasure. He went on to explain that historians had, at various times, placed him in China, Ethiopia, and the steppes of Russia. "With that background, and a good deal of imagination, you can visualize this as a medieval map of the world. The many Christian fish symbols represent his kingdoms, and the larger three fish, we believe the sites of his own palaces."

"Yes," said Rid. "Note the three larger fish. One in China, where this map was found. One in what is now Ethiopia, and one north of Kiev, in the Russian steppes."

"I'm convinced that Presterman will want to see these. Let's go with your plan. The Prime Minister has offered our help in any way we can," Evelyn announced.

"I got the same offer from our President, with a note of caution," Bryan broke in. "After my initial report, the President summoned his advisors. The Secretary of the Treasury was concerned about a stock market collapse in utility stocks if these facts are true. And his political advisors reminded the President of the extent of his campaign contributions from the energy industry."

"I need to call the President to cover my part in this," Yager said. "If it does go wrong, I need to make sure he understands I was just here because of the China connection."

"If we are right, then Treasury and the President better start working on plan B," Rid admonished.

"We are right!" Milt said emphatically. "We will keep you posted as to our progress."

THIRTY-ONE

London and Rome

The next morning it was foggy and drizzling all over the British Isles. Bryan Robert had a U.S. Air Force limousine pick him up at Dukes Hotel as he was to fly back to Washington that day aboard one of the big C5 cargo planes that made regular runs to supply the bases in Europe. He asked if Rid and Milt would like to ride with him so they could meet the courier from Beijing who was bringing the original map pictures. Then the car could take them to Heathrow for their commercial flight back to Rome. They wanted to stop there first to review the case with Monsignor Corso and to plan their approach to a meeting with Presterman.

When they got to the air base they found all traffic had been delayed, waiting on the fog to lift above the minimum ceiling for landing.

While they waited in the departure area, Bryan asked, "How do you plan to arrange a meeting with Presterman, or Floyd, or what the hell else name he might be using?"

"We haven't finished our plan yet, Bryan," Rid replied. "One thought I had was to simply walk into his offices in New York and see if he shows up. We would recognize each other instantly."

"That could be dangerous," reminded the CIA Deputy Director. "Remember how ruthless he was in his last attempt to make himself king of the world."

"I've been thinking about it, too," Milt interjected. "I think it's time for the two of us to have a face-to-face with this Professor O'Brien who acted as Floyd's front man in hiring us. We can tell him we have some exciting news that we want to share with his employer. Show him the pictures and tell him more about our skirmishes with the Defenders."

"How does that get us to Presterman? Won't he just say that he will report for us?" Rid challenged.

"Not if we tell O'Brien to specifically tell his boss that a friend recommended we call him," Milt started.

"And that friend would be?" Bryan interrupted.

"Dean Floyd, of course," Milt answered with a grin.

"That could work," Rid said. If we phrase it right, he will know we know who he is and that we are coming as a friend. We convinced him for a while in the last caper that I was on his side. We can do it again."

"It's worth a shot," Bryan said. "Go for it!"

The flight from Beijing finally arrived at 11 AM, four hours late. They were surprised when Bob Bell got off the plane, leading Liu Chow Lim down the stairs. "Hello," he yelled. "I have brought the pictures and your guide."

"What happened?" Rid asked as he gave Liu a big hug.

She said, "The police wanted to question me further, and Mr. Bell interceded on my behalf Then they decided I could go as long as I left China."

"She has ask for asylum. I told her we would take care of her," Bell said.

"Liu is happy to see the two of you," she said to Milt and Rid.

"As we are to see you safe," Milt replied.

Bryan said, "I can take her with me to Washington and put her into our immigration program."

"I have a better idea, Bryan, if you agree," Rid began. "Let her go with us to Rome. She can work for us at Janus International. She has a great deal of expertise in Marco Polo and his search for the original Prester John."

"That's fine by me. What about when the case is over?"

"One of three things," Rid answered. "If we find the treasure of Prester John and return it to the Chinese government, they will give her a hero's welcome and she can go home. If not, she can choose between the United States or stay in Italy and continue to work for us. We need someone to manage our office."

"He's right about that, Bryan," Milt added. "You know we field-trained operatives are horrendous at keeping up with the office."

"Yeah. I have several hundred of that kind working for me now," Bryan said. "Liu, you heard their offer. Do you want to go to Rome?"

"Yes please, I would like to continue the search," she eagerly replied.

As Bryan Robert's plane was lifting off on its flight to Washington, Rid, Liu, and Milt were being driven to Heathrow Airport. Once there, they bought tickets on the next British Air flight to Rome. It was leaving in 25 minutes, so they hurried to the gate. When they landed at Rome's Fiumicino Airport a little over two hours later, it was a bright, sunny, warm day.

They went to their office and found it trashed. It had been thoroughly searched.

"Defenders, probably," Milt said.

'No doubt," echoed Rid. "Maybe Bengali sent word about the pictures before we killed him."

"It looks that way. Let's see what's missing."

They searched the office, but nothing of importance had been taken. Rid turned to Liu and said, "We told you our office was a mess, but never like this."

"It is all right. I will straighten it out," she assured them.

"We can't leave you here alone," Rid said. "You can stay at my place until we find one for you. I will sleep here at the office in case the intruders return. Here are my keys, Milt. Please take her to my apartment for the night. Every thing she needs is there."

"Okay. Let's meet with Ricardo tomorrow and tell him about the pictures and introduce him to Liu," Milt proposed.

"Good idea. The two of them, together with the Vatican's library may help solve the puzzle of our friend P.J.," Rid answered. "I'll call him and set a time for in the morning. After we meet with Corso, we will call this Randall O'Brien to set a meeting with him."

"The sooner, the better," Milt said. "I have a strong feeling we are getting closer to both Prester John and Johnathan Presterman."

THIRTY-TWO

Rome

Taylor had an uneventful night sleeping in the office. He felt certain the Defenders of the Faith of Prester John were watching the place and would have seen the lights. But nobody came. Milt arrived at 8:30 with Liu.

"How was your night, Rid?" he asked.

"Quiet!" he replied. "How about you?"

"I took Liu to dinner with my Louise to La Sacresta for pasta," Milt explained. "Then we took her to your place. Louise loaned her some clothes."

"Your getting pretty serious with Louise, Milt. Am I soon to be a partner-in-law?" Rid quipped.

"I'm trying to get her to say yes to becoming Louise Young, but she says I'm always gone. Someday, I'll win her over."

"So, Ridley. How do I look?" Liu asked.

"Very Western and very beautiful," he responded.

Liu blushed and said with a grin, "Do I look Italian?"

"Not quite," Rid answered. "But then there are many different cultures here in Rome. I know you will like it here."

"What about our meeting with the Monsignor?" Milt changed the subject.

"We are set for ten this morning. Ricardo seemed most excited at meeting Liu. He thinks their pooled knowledge may help pinpoint Prester John."

"Until we go to see him," Liu began. "Let's finish cleaning up this place. It is a mess."

While cleaning and putting files back together they discussed what to do about the Defenders. They decided to alert the police and their own building security firm. Milt scoured the office for bugs, but none were found. They each retrieved firearms from their safe and put on shoulder holsters. The time passed quickly until it was time to leave for the Vatican. They arrived at the employees entrance at five minutes to ten, checked their guns with the guard, and went up to the Curator's office on the fifth floor.

Corso rose from his desk, arms outstretched, and came toward them. "You must be Professor Liu Chow Lim, from Sun Yat Sen University in Beijing. It is a distinct pleasure to have you here."

"The honor is mine," Liu said with a bow. "It's Assistant Professor. I am very excited at the prospect of working with such a distinguished scholar."

"And work we will. Just as soon as we get these two on their way," Corso agreed.

"Were still being chased by the Defenders of P.J. So we're not going anywhere until we know she is safe," Rid stated.

"I can solve that," Ricardo offered. "We have many extra rooms within the Vatican for visitors. I'll arrange one for her. She will be completely safe here. "

"That's great. That will free us to go to the states to expose this Johnathan Presterman," Milt beamed. "We need to go to Maine and then New York, so it could take a few days."

"I'll get her a pass to the employee cafeteria and one for the use of our Library. She can use that empty office in the far corner for her work. And I will watch over her."

With Liu's safety assured, Ridley and Milt reviewed everything that happened in China. When they discussed the mosaic map and got out the photographs, the Monsignor became obviously excited.

"These pictures are extremely important to the history of the Christian religion. I must have copies made for us," he said.

"You should keep the original set. If we find we are meeting with the evil Dean Floyd, he may have us killed to get them."

"I can have copies made here within thirty minutes," Ricardo said as he took the photos out to his aide. As he returned, he went on, "You know, I have James Marblestone, the forger from Hebrew University still on my staff. If you like, I'm sure he could use his computer to alter the photos. That would make it less likely the precise locations of the map symbols could be determined."

"I like the way you think, Ricardo," Rid agreed. "We will take Liu to get her things. Is it all right to bring her back this afternoon after we make our trip arrangements?"

"Certainly. The doctored photos will be ready any time after two."

The trio went first to Ridley's apartment to pack a small bag with the clothes Louise had given her. They also went to a *farmicia* to get toiletries, and to a dry goods place for towels, sheets, and the like. They paused for lunch at Vente Tres, near the Trevi Fountain. The pizze margherita and capellini with a very light fresh pomodoro sauce were excellent. At two they returned to the Vatican Museum.

"I see, Liu, that you are ready to move in. Might I suggest that we get you to your room so you can rest today? I will call for you at seven. I have arranged for dinner in our Cardinal's dining room with some of my colleagues. They are the ones with whom you will be working."

"I am most thankful, your Eminence," she said.

"Save that Eminence stuff for the Pope. I've become used to Ricardo since becoming involved with your two protectors," Corso admonished.

"Yes Father, I mean Ricardo."

The Monsignor's aide, a young nun, came in and escorted Liu to her quarters in the convent. She marveled at the beauty of the stained glass along the way. Her room had a small window overlooking the Vatican's gardens. There was a small bed, a table, a chair, a set of drawers, and a wash stand. The bathroom and showers were down the hall. Liu told her escort, "This will be fine. Compared to many places in China, this is wonderful."

"Thank you. If you need anything, dial 2714 on the phone in the hall. That is my extension. Monsignor Corso is 2713. He says he will send for you at seven." She left her alone.

Though somewhat bewildered by all that had happened to her over the last few days, Liu felt safe and excited about searching for Prester John. She wished there was a way she could tell Dr. Wu what was going on.

Back in the Museum office, Rid was telling Ricardo that they were on the next day's Alitalia flight to Boston. "Clark and Lyn are going to meet us and drive us to their new place in south Portland, Maine. They are to call this Professor O'Brien and arrange a meeting for us the next day. He is the entree to Floyd."

"Good luck and stay alert, my friends."

"You can count on that," Rid said.

"There is one other thing about this, Ricardo. I feel our escapades in China are going to reflect negatively on the Vatican's relations with their legation here in Rome," Milt explained.

"You let us worry about that. If these photos help convince our Foreign Affairs Committee that there was a real Presbyter in China, I'm sure we will fund an expedition to explore the site."

"That would be great. It would give Liu a chance to return home," Milt said.

Rid added, "There is a Professor Wu, at the University in Beijing, who is trying to raise money for such a project. Liu studied under him and he is the one who let us take these pictures."

"Sounds like it may all come together nicely. Now be on your way and beard this Presterman in his den," Corso closed the conversation.

As the two were getting in a taxi outside the Vatican, Milt said. "I hope when we beard him, the Vatican's lights don't go out with the rest of the world."

"Floyd doesn't have that much control of electric power yet," Rid argued.

"*Yet* is the key word. Each day he gets closer to his dream of world power by controlling the world's power supply," Milt left that thought with Rid when the taxi dropped him at his apartment.

There was a message on his answer machine from the police. He was to call Lieutenant Borio at the main station. He dialed the number.

"Prego," the voice answered.

"Buona sera. Lieutenant Borio, please."

"Ah, anglais. This is Lieutenant Borio. You are?" he left the question dangling.

"Ridley Taylor. You left a message for me to call."

"Yes. We have good news. Today on a patrol of your offices, my men captured two thugs who had broken in. Would you like to see them?"

"Are they wearing dark suits and ties?" Rid asked.

"Yes and they were armed with curved daggers."

"I'm on my way. Where are they being held?"

"The central jail on Via Repubblica."

"I know it. I'll call my partner, and we'll be there within the hour."

Rid hung up and immediately dialed Milt's cell phone.

"Young here," he answered.

"Where are you?" Rid started. "The police are holding two of the Defenders at the jail. They captured them outside our office."

"I'm at the office now, picking up our tickets and passports for tomorrow's flight. Nothing seems out of place; but, then, I'm not used to seeing this place so neat. It's hard for me to tell if something is missing."

"Where were our tickets?

"On my desk. Uh-oh. You think they might have seen where we are going, Rid?"

"I think we will soon know if the Defenders of Prester John's faith have a chapter in the United States."

THIRTY-THREE

Rome and Boston

Rid and Milt arrived at the central jail within five minutes of each other. They were each escorted to Lieutenant Borio's office where they waited another fifteen minutes for the detective to return from the interrogation rooms.

"We have separated the two and have begun questioning them. So far, neither has said a word," Borio began. "Who are they?"

Milt answered, "We would have to see them to be sure, but from your description, they are part of a cult named Defenders of the Faith of Prester John."

"I never heard of him. Tell me more."

Rid and Milt told him the story of the mysterious Prester John and of the killings in Ethiopia, China, and Rome. They omitted any reference to Johnathan Presterman. Then Rid said, "Perhaps if we join in your interrogation, they will know we have shared with you our conflict with them. They may become more talkative."

"It's worth a try," the Lieutenant said as he led them out of the office. When they arrived at the separate holding rooms, Borio took Milt into the first room and introduced him to Detective

Antonio Rossi, who was leading the interrogation. He then took Rid with him into the second room. Rid took one look, and said, "I've seen this man before. He is the one who escaped the day they shot up our office last month. You can put murder on his arrest sheet. I'll gladly testify."

With that the previously silent prisoner started babbling about how the killing was done by this American and his partner. "I am the victim," he said.

"Don't listen to that. You caught them breaking in to our office again today. If you want corroboration, call Captain Hakeem Olajoni in Addis Ababa, Ethiopia. He will tell you of the deaths in his country caused by these thugs."

Meanwhile, Milt experienced a somewhat different scenario. His prisoner was the one he saw in Venice after he had lost his turban at the church of San Georgio. He immediately said he would speak only to a court-appointed attorney.

"You may not know that the priest you stabbed, Father Cesar Saputo, survived. He also can identify you. At the least, Detective Rossi, you can charge him with attempted murder along with breaking and entering, carrying a concealed weapon, and whatever else you can come up with."

"Do not worry, my friend. It will be a long time before this one is back on the street," Rossi assured him.

After a short wrap-up visit, where Rid told the police they were flying to the United States the next day. They were allowed to leave the jail.

"Please let me know when you return to Rome, Signori," he said.

"We will," Milt answered. "It should be within ten days."

"Prego. Ciao!"

"Ciao," they replied.

The next morning, they took the flight to Boston, arriving at 3:25 PM local time. Clark and Lyn Keene were outside the arrival hall to meet them.

"Hello," Clark yelled while waving. "Welcome to Boston."

"Thanks. We only have these carry-on bags, so we can leave right away," Rid said as he hurried them out of Logan Airport. Once at the car, he added, "We were probably being watched, as the Defenders knew our flight."

"I didn't see anything unusual," Clark countered.

"What about that blind Arab with the seeing-eye dog, Clark," Lyn said, "He had been hanging around for a long time."

"To be safe, let's take Route 1, instead of the interstate," Rid cautioned.

"Do they know where we live?" Lyn began to worry. "We just moved last week from our home in Cape Elizabeth to a waterside condo in south Portland."

"I remember you calling the office last week," Milt said. "I changed your address in our files, so they probably know your new location. Is there any other place you can stay?"

"We could go to our son, Danny's, place in Hallowell. It's up by Augusta," Clark offered.

"Good. Milt and I can house-sit your place. Do you have any weapons?"

"I have an old Browning twelve-gauge shotgun and a pellet target pistol," came the reply.

"That will do. Now tell us about Professor O'Brien," Milt said.

"He is planning on seeing you in his office at Bowdoin University tomorrow at three. He has classes till then," Clark answered.

"That's fine. We'll need a car," Milt continued.

"You can use my all-wheel-drive Subaru," Lyn offered.

"Great. Now drop us off at your place and pick up what you need for Denny's," Milt requested.

"It's Danny's," Clark corrected.

"Yeah, Danny's. Don't try to call us. Your lines have probably been tapped," Rid admonished.

The Keenes' new condo was on Anchorage Place, right on Casco Bay. It overlooked downtown Portland across the bay. It was two levels. The lower level was garage and entry way. The living quarters were on the second floor, which made an excellent defensive position.

After the Keenes had left for Hallowell, Ridley and Milt cleaned the two guns they found. They loaded both and put them on the dining room table. They turned out the lights, made sandwiches, and ate them in the dark.

"I'll take the first shift, Milt. You get some sleep. I'll wake you up at midnight."

"Okay. I have a strong feeling we will have visitors before this night is over."

"I do, too, Milt, I do, too."

THIRTY-FOUR

South Portland

It was the middle of Ridley Taylor's watch, around 2:30 AM, that he heard a noise out on the second story deck off the living room. He crossed silently in the dark to the sliding glass door. A rope with a treble hook had been thrown over the railing. It was pulled taut as if someone was climbing the rope. Rid slid open the door and fired the shotgun out over the bay. The rope immediately went slack. Rid raced to the deck's edge. He saw two black-clad figures running around the end of the building and then heard a car speeding away.

As he reentered the room, Milt came out of the bedroom saying, "What was that?"

"Our visitors showed up and were trying to scale the balcony. They don't like the noise of a shotgun. They're gone."

"It seems some of the Keenes' neighbors didn't like the sound either. Do you hear those police sirens coming closer?"

Rid suggested, "Let's just tell the police that someone was trying to break in and I fired the shot to scare them away."

"That's the truth," Milt agreed.

They went outside to meet the arriving police. Rid explained what had happened. Then he took them around to the water side of the budding and showed them the rope hanging from the balcony. The patrolmen called for a crime scene crew. When they arrived some fifteen minutes later, they began making plaster casts of footprints and dusting for fingerprints on the rope and the wood-shingled walls.

South Portland's Police Chief, Jim Orr, also came to the scene. He took Rid and Milt back inside and had Rid repeat the story.

"Do you think this was just an attempted robbery?" the Chief asked.

"That's my guess," Rid answered. "We are not from here, however. We are house-sitting for friends, Clark and Lyn Keene."

"I thought this was their place. They just moved here from Cape Elizabeth. Right?"

"That's right," Milt said. "The Keenes are on our company's board of directors."

"And what company is that?" Orr asked.

Rid explained, "We are called Janus International. We do security reviews for large companies and search for long lost things."

"Sounds like interesting work, How do you prepare for such a unique career?" the Chief continued.

"We want to be straight with you, Chief Orr," Milt said.

Orr interrupted, "Call me Jim. That's how I'm known in the area."

"Okay, Jim. You'll find when you check our backgrounds that I was an agent for British Intelligence. Ridley was the same for your CIA."

"It's feeling more and more like this may not have been a simple home burglary," Orr surmised.

"We may as well tell you everything, Jim. Rather than have you have to dig it out piece by piece," Rid began.

Over the next hour, Rid and Milt told the entire story of the Keenes' initial visit with Professor O'Brien, to the killings in Rome, Ethiopia, and China.

About the time they finished the story, one of the Chief s deputies came in and whispered something in the Chief s ear.

"I already know who they are. They told me they used to be in the spy game. Anything else, Peter?"

"The team is puzzled by some of the plaster footprints. They appear to be made by a pointed toe slipper of some kind," he said aloud.

"That would be members of the Defenders of the Faith of Prester John that we told you about. They seem to be everywhere."

"We'll issue arrest warrants for them. Are they dangerous?" Jim wanted to know.

"Extremely. Their favorite weapon is a curved dagger like you see in old movies about Arab countries. We believe these people are from India."

"Okay, Peter. Get on it," Jim ordered.

After the deputy was gone, the Chief glared at the two so-called victims, and asked, "So, why didn't you tell me all this the first time I asked?"

"We thought it was better to keep quiet about what really happened. An attempted break-in would sit a lot better with the neighbors than some Indian thugs with daggers roaming the neighborhood," Milt responded.

"We half expected we were followed here from Rome. That's why we had the Keenes go to their son's house in Hallowell," Rid added.

"What about the shotgun? Is it yours?" the Chief continued.

"It belongs to Clark Keene. We are not carrying guns, even though we are fully licensed to do so."

"What is the real purpose of your visit, and how long will you be here?" Orr asked.

"We came to meet with Professor O'Brien at Bowdoin College. That is set for tomorrow afternoon. We will probably go on to New York after the meeting," Milt answered.

"Good. Let me suggest several things. International crime is nonexistent here in South Portland. I will report this as a simple burglary attempt. We will also keep a close watch on this place until you are out of Maine. Finally, let me help you obtain legal weapons within your permits. I'm guessing that your dagger-wielding friends will follow you to New York.

"That all sounds great. You are a talented policeman. We'll remember what you have done to help," Rid thanked Orr.

"My thanks will come when you get out of here without further incidents," the Chief replied.

"We only control half the equation, Jim. We'll make sure they know we are going on to New York. They have access to flight passenger lists," Milt said.

The Chief left after Rid and Milt had agreed to meet him again at ten that morning, They were to sign written statements covering the night's activities. They also were to select handguns the Police Department had for sale to licensed law enforcement officers. The guns were from a large inventory of confiscated weapons seized from criminals.

After he left, Milt said, "I like him."

"Me, too. He's smart," Rid agreed. "Now let's get a little sleep. It's five in the morning."

THIRTY-FIVE

South Portland

Ridley was awake first around 8:15. He showered, dressed, and put in a call to the Keenes at their son's home in Hallowell. Danny answered. "Dan's Haunted House. Come stay a night."

"This is Ridley Taylor, Dan. Is your mom or dad there?"

"They're both right here, sipping tea and hot chocolate and watching the Weather Channel."

"Let me talk to your dad."

A moment later, Clark Keene was on the line. "How did it go, Rid?"

"We had visitors, as we suspected. They tried to scale your balcony. Your shotgun scared them off when I fired it out over the bay."

"Wow, what happened then?"

"Your neighbors were up and the police came. Chief Orr, Milt, and I had a long discussion about our case. He has offered to help by watching your place and helping us get some better weapons. He wants you to stay in Hallowell until we are out of Maine, taking the thugs with us."

"Do the neighbors know the truth?"

"No. The Chief agreed we should report this as an attempted break-in. The rest isn't public knowledge."

"What's your next move?" Keene asked.

Rid explained, "We have to go to the police station at ten to sign a written statement and pick up the guns. Our meeting with the Professor at Bowdoin is at three this afternoon. If that works out, we'll leave for New York after the meeting."

"Why don't you come by here for lunch. It's not far out of the way. You can drive here in just over an hour and it's less than that from here to Bowdoin. The Weather Channel says it may start snowing this evening, so you should be okay" Clark offered.

"Good idea. We can fill you in on the details then. Milt and I haven't discussed our travel arrangements. I think we should rent a car to drive all the way to New York. We may be able to lose our followers that way."

"Okay. We'll see you about noon. Take the turnpike north to exit 17. That's State Route 9. Follow it for four miles to Hallowell. Dan's house is the first driveway past the flashing yellow light."

"We'll be there," Rid closed the conversation. As he was hanging up the phone, Milt entered the room.

"I got most of that. We're driving to Hallowell, then to Bowdoin, and then to New York?" he asked.

"Less chance of being followed that way, partner."

"That's true. But we promised Chief Orr we would make sure the Defenders knew we were leaving."

Rid replied, "Not a problem. They should have someone watching the Portland Airport who will see us rent a car. I'll use my regular credit card so they can get a record of the car, license, and destination."

"If they have all that, just how do you plan to elude them?" Milt chided.

"They'll assume we went toward the stated destination, New York. We go south first, then east, then north. Later, when we get to Boston, there are several interstates that get you to the city."

"Hope you're right. We better get ready, Rid, for our trip to the police station. "

"Yeah. First, let me call Orr to see if he will pick us up and then take us to the airport. That way we can leave Lyn's Subaru here," Rid said.

Chief Orr pulled up to the front of the condo at 9:50. Rid and Milt were waiting by the garage, where they had been talking to some of the neighbors. They had explained the police thought it was a botched robbery attempt.

"Good morning, Jim," Milt greeted the Chief.

"Yep! Nice this morning. Talking about snow later. You two sleep any?"

"We each had two hours before the ruckus, and about three more this morning, so we're okay," Rid reported. "How about you?"

Orr replied, "Not so fortunate. I've been up all night, trying to get a line on these Defenders. I did call Captain Olajoni in Ethiopia. He confirmed your story," Orr said as he backed out of the drive. He went on, "I also reached a Lieutenant Borio in Rome. He said to tell you he was still holding the two that were caught in your office."

"Good," Milt said. "We are sorry we brought this international conspiracy to your town."

"I'd have to say I like days with nothing but traffic problems better, but this brings some excitement to an otherwise dull existence," Jim said as he pulled in to his reserved space at the station,

The session went quickly. The chief had prepared two versions of the crime. One for the public record of an attempted robbery. The other the true version, Rid and Milt signed off on both. Then the Chief took them to the station's firing range. There were a few officers shooting at targets. Off to the side was a locked cage that contained confiscated weapons. There were all types, from machine guns to automatics to police specials. Milt found his favorite, a Walther PPK. Having been in British Intelligence, he thought it was his duty to use the same weapon as the famous James Bond. Ridley wanted a little more power. He picked a .45-caliber automatic. Then the Chief drove the two to the airport.

On the way, Ridley explained their plan for renting a car and making certain the bad guys could get the information so they would leave the area. Milt added their plans for Hallowell and Bowdoin with their expected schedule.

At the airport, the Chief said, "I'm going to give you a two-minute head start. Then I want to come in to see if I can spot a watcher."

"Okay. They may have already seen us get out of your car, so they may be out of sight," Milt warned.

"I'll have a look anyway."

As the two approached the Hertz counter, a black-clad figure put down his newspaper and went out the side parking lot door. He was gone before the Chief entered the terminal. After the paperwork was done, they said goodbye to their new friend and went out to their car.

The Chief was watching them drive away when he saw a dark-colored sedan pull in behind them on to the turnpike.

THIRTY-SIX

Rome

While Taylor and Young were at the South Portland Police Station, evening was approaching in Rome. Liu Chow Lim had immersed herself in the Vatican Library's material about Prester John. She also cross-referenced the locations from that source with another file on early Christian missionaries who were in Africa, Asia, and India. It was in that file she found another reference to the Presbyter. She quickly took the file to the Curator's office.

"Look what I have found," she said proudly. "A new reference to Prester John."

"Let's have a look Liu. Where did you find it?" Corso became excited.

"In a file on early missionaries. The piece was written in the early thirteenth century by a monk scholar who was at the Kells monastery in Ireland," she went on.

"That's an important thing to know. At Trinity College in Dublin, they display part of the *Book of Kells*. It's a very old translation of the Bible. It's like the Dead Sea Scrolls with some verses not in the versions done in the Middle Ages. What does it say about Prester John?" the Monsignor asked.

Liu explained, "It speculates as to his being a real person or a hoax. Remember, the early thirteenth century would be only about forty years after Prester John sent his letter to Emperor Manuel I in Byzantium."

"What was the writer's conclusion?" Corso eagerly asked.

"That he did exist, that he did write the letter promising to bring a large army to win back the Holy Land," she summarized. "But at the time of the monk's study, he said no army had come forth."

"Then it must have been very early in the century, as Genghis Khan did his conquering from about 1210 to 1225. This may support Marco Polo's thesis that Khan killed Prester John and used his fortune to support his vast army."

Liu continued, "The study also speculates on the location of the Prester's palace. It has all the places, Janus has on its list: Ethiopia, the Three Indias, Peking, Samarkand in the Russian steppes, plus it adds one more."

"Where is that?" Ricardo urged her on.

"A place called the Great Zimbabwe farther south in Africa. I looked it up in a book on ancient civilizations. It's in southern Africa in the country called Zimbabwe today. It was a very cultured, learned society that existed for about 400 years and then vanished, much like the Mayans of Central America. They were great builders and astronomers. They understood mathematics, the seasons, and changed from being hunters always on the move to growers of crops and livestock."

"All very interesting, Liu. Does the writer say why he listed this place as one of the locations for Prester John?"

"Only that the main structure, which was called the Great Zimbabwe, is large enough to house such a palace, with it's required dormitories, places of worship, stables, dining halls, and so on. It also has an ample water supply from the Zambezi River. What do you think, Father?"

"Ricardo, please. I think this is a major new development. I'm certain Milt and Ridley will want to go there. I'll do some checking to see if there has been any archeological activities there. Rid or Milt should be calling in within the next few days. I'll have you explain your find. You did a wonderful job on this. You are the kind of researcher I like to have on my staff. Maybe you should stay in Rome and come work for the Museum."

"I'd like that. But only until China gets funding for a new dig at the site near Beijing. I promised Dr. Wu I would assist him there."

"Fair enough. For now, see what else you find on the Zimbabwe site."

"Yes, Ricardo," Liu beamed her beautiful smile.

THIRTY-SEVEN

Hallowell

Milt spotted the trailing car just after entering the turnpike. He said to Rid, "Looks like we have company."

"How far back?" Rid asked.

"I'd call it 100 yards. Maybe they want us to see them," Milt suggested.

"Let's lose them now, Milt."

With that, Milt increased their speed to over eighty miles per hour, passed a semi-trailer truck on the right, and then did a U turn across the grassy median. The other car was passing the truck when Milt crossed the median. By the time the chasing car realized what had happened and made their own U turn, Milt was exiting the highway at the same interchange they had just entered. The man at the toll was puzzled by their ticket. It showed them entering only a few minutes earlier.

"We went the wrong way," Milt explained. "Sorry,"

"Okay. No charge," the man in the booth said as he raised the gate. Milt then pulled over behind two trucks that were parked by the turnpike office. They watched as the two in the black car came through the gate and drove down to the street. After a pause, they turned right, back toward the airport. Milt then pulled across the line of toll booths, got a new ticket, and reentered the highway.

"By the time they figure out what happened we should be forty miles ahead. Good work, partner."

"Thanks, Rid. To be sure, I'll get off the highway at Freeport and take the back roads to Hallowell."

When they exited at Freeport there were dozens of cars doing the same thing.

"Everyone is going to L. L. Bean," Rid said.

"Sure looks that way. They should turn right at the corner. Our road is left, away from town," Milt replied.

The rest of the trip was uneventful. Rid called the Keenes on his cell phone as they were approaching Hallowell, to say they were almost there. When they arrived, Clark and Lyn were standing out in front.

"Welcome!" Clark said as Lyn gave each of them a hug.

"Thanks. We started out with company. I think we lost them," Milt told the story of the toll booths.

"Put your car in the garage and come on in," Clark suggested,

The house was a large two-and-a-half-story Victorian, with a separate apartment on one side. It sat on top of a hill and overlooked the Kennebunk River. With lace curtains on the widows and a lot of gingerbread moldings, it could pass as a haunted house. As they entered, the Keenes' son Danny was in the kitchen, making lasagna. He paused to wipe his hands and welcome his guests.

"What's with the 'Haunted House' business, Dan?" Rid asked.

"The lady I . . . oops . . . Mom, Dad, and I bought it from told me she had heard noises and had seen shadows a number of times over the years she lived here," Danny explained.

"The other day you answered the phone suggesting your callers come stay a night. You using this as a bed-and-breakfast?" Rid probed.

"I'm working toward that. I'm remodeling the upstairs so each bedroom will have a bathroom. I do the work myself, so it will be a while before it's done. In the meantime me and my answering machine are doing a little promoting. I already have two reservations for next Halloween," Dan answered proudly.

"Halloween in Hallowell," Milt quipped. "Not bad, Danny."

Dan returned to his cooking while Rid and Milt went over the story about the attempted break-in at their condo. They covered everything they had discussed with the police and Chief Jim Orr.

"I know Orr," Clark said. "He's a good man."

"He sure helped us," Rid said. "Now, go over again all you know about this Professor O'Brien. You met with him several times."

"That's right," Lyn started. "We first met him when he brought the news of the Fuhrwerks' deaths in Ethiopia. That's when he asked us to contact you about finding Prester John's treasure."

Clark interrupted, "That's also when he told us about his anonymous backer."

The Keenes alternately told of their other contacts with O'Brien. When Janus accepted the case, when they were trying to decipher the Defenders of the Faith initials, when they gave him weekly progress reports, and when they set up the meeting for this afternoon.

"What's he like?" Milt asked.

"Very personable. Not at all like you would expect a medieval history professor at Bowdoin to be," Lyn said.

"Athletic. I hear he is a very good golfer," Clark added. "Short and slender. Smart."

"Do you think he knows the identity of his backer?" Rid posed the big question.

"He certainly knows how to get messages to him. He has done that a number of times," Clark replied.

"We'll ask him this afternoon," Milt said.

A car pulled into the drive. Lyn looked out the window and said, "It's our daughter, Kerry."

Lyn went to the door and let Kerry in. "What are you doing here, Ker?"

"Dan told me he was making lasagna. School closed early today because of the snow forecast, so I thought I would get something good to eat."

Kerry was a student of speech therapy at the University of Rhode Island. She was a very attractive single woman who had decided to come for the weekend.

"Time to eat!" Danny yelled from the kitchen. He had set up a buffet on the kitchen counter. Lasagna, salad, and homemade bread sticks. Bardolino red and Frascati white wines were on the table. Empty water glasses were there for the wines. "Mom and Dad say you enjoy the same wines we like. Who got it from who?"

"I think your mother told us about them first," Rid answered. "Your dad calls them the Keene family ancestral wines. We order them faithfully when we are in Rome."

Over lunch, Rid, Milt, and the senior Keenes quizzed the two thirtysomethings about what was happening in their lives. No serious love interests for either of them. That disappointed Lyn, who was looking forward to being a grandmother.

"That lasagna was really good, Dan. Maybe you could open a restaurant in Rome. Milt and I would be your best patrons," Rid said as he finished his second portion.

"I agree," Milt echoed. "We need to get going to our meeting with the Professor. Come on Rid."

They said their goodbyes. Once in the car, Milt said, "What a nice family. I sure hope we haven't put them in danger."

They drove on toward Bowdoin and their meeting with Professor O'Brien.

THIRTY-EIGHT

Brunswick, Maine

Rid and Milt arrived at Bowdoin College with fifteen minutes left to find Professor O'Brien's office. They pulled into the visitor parking area and walked toward the main buildings. The third student they asked pointed toward the History Building and said, "Professor O'Brien is on the second floor, room 217.

"Thanks!" Milt said. They went into the building and found O'Brien's office. No one was there and the door was locked.

"It's not quite three. Maybe he is still in class," Rid suggested.

Before Milt could answer, the end-of-class buzzer sounded and the hall immediately filled with students. A trim-looking teacher came out of the classroom directly across the hall. He crossed over and said, "You must be Taylor and Young from Janus. I'm Randy O'Brien."

"Nice to meet you in person. We've only been in touch through the Keenes," Rid answered. "I'm Rid Taylor. He's Milt Young."

"Call me Randy. Come on in."

It was a small office with a desk pushed in one corner and a small table with four chairs near the window. There was clutter everywhere. Stacks of paper and books covered the table and the desk. O'Brien cleared an area on the table by putting those items on top of those on the desk. He motioned for his visitors to sit. "How can I help?" he asked.

"We have made a significant discovery in the search for the treasure of Prester John," Milt began. "We want to meet with your backer to discuss our next moves. It could involve significantly more expense."

"I don't know whether he would meet with you. My instructions have been very clear. No personal contact between him and anyone involved in the search," the Professor was adamant.

"Let me lay it out for you. Then you can ask him whether he'll see us," Rid said as he removed the photographs from the envelope. "These pictures are a part of the mosaic tile floor of a palace near Beijing. The photographs were taken of an old drawing made by Marco Polo. It is the site that Polo believed was the court of Prester John. Look close. Do you see several outlines of the ancient Christian fish symbol?"

"Yes, I see them. That would substantiate Polo's conclusion," he said in an excited tone. "What else was at the site?"

"Lots of ruins," Milt took over. There have been limited digs at the site because the Chinese government doesn't want to spend the money to finance a major excavation. That's why we want to meet with Mr. Anonymous."

"I don't know," the Professor mused.

"Look a little closer," Rid said. "Note that three of the fish are larger than the others. Prester John's original letter said he had seventy-two kings under him. From the small parts of the floor visible in these pictures, it appears there could easily be seventy-two fish. And note that three of the fish in the second picture are larger than the others. One is the site at Beijing, one in Ethiopia where the Fuhrwerks were digging, and one north of Kiev, in the Russian steppes."

"This really is exciting. All of this seems to validate the fact that there really was a Prester John. I know my backer will want to see these pictures. Why don't I take them to him, along with an estimate of the costs to explore the three main sites? Then I'll report his answer to you."

"No deal," Milt interrupted. "We've been shot at, stabbed, and chased everywhere we've been on this case. You remember telling the Keenes about the cult that calls themselves the Defenders of the Faith of Prester John?."

"Yes. Are they still a problem?" O'Brien asked.

"It wouldn't at all surprise me if some of them aren't here on campus," Milt responded. "You could be in serious danger if you tried to take these pictures to your benefactor yourself."

"I don't like that," O'Brien said as he gazed out the window. "Look, by the tree in the middle of the quad. Those two in black suits are not students. Could they be some of the Defenders you fear?" he asked with trepidation.

"Certainly! As a novice at our kind of work, you could lead these thugs directly to your boss. We can get there without the tail," Milt explained.

"I'll call him now and see if he will meet with you," the Professor said. "Please wait in the hall."

"One more thing. Tell your sponsor we have already met with a man named Dean Floyd and have him on standby for the Ethiopian dig," Rid added to the reasons for a personal visit.

While the Professor was on the phone, Milt and Rid went down to the main door and stood outside long enough to be spotted by the waiting Defenders. Then they went back upstairs and waited inside the first classroom at the top of the stairs. They heard the shuffle of the intruders' feet, opened the door as they passed, and pressed gun barrels into their backs. "Easy now," Rid said calmly. "Drop your daggers to the floor." They prodded them into the empty classroom. "Sit in those seats. I'll watch these two. Find something to tie them up."

Milt found video and electric cables all across the front of the classroom. He bound them tightly to their chairs. Near the door was a Lost and Found box full of knit hats and scarves the students used during the cold Maine winters. He stuffed a hat in each thug's mouth and tied a scarf around their head to silence them.

Then they went back to the Professor's office. "Sorry, we went to see about the two in black coats. They may not look like students but they are really tied to their desks right now," Rid quipped.

"Will your benefactor meet with us?" Milt asked.

"He was reluctant at first, until I told him about you meeting with this Dean Floyd. Then he immediately said yes. He wants you in New York by two tomorrow afternoon. You are to call Samuel Gold, a partner at Richards and Clark. He will tell you the arrangements for the meeting."

"Thank you, Randy. We'll leave for the city right away," Milt said. "One piece of business for you, Randy. Wait about fifteen minutes, then call campus security and have them take the two intruders in room 202 to jail. They are wanted in South Portland for several crimes. Have your police contact Jim Orr. He is the Chief of Police there."

"Where are they?" O'Brien asked.

Rid replied, "Room 202. Sitting in the back row, bound and gagged. Here is one of their daggers." He put it on the table.

"This is priceless. Looks to be genuine fourteenth or fifteenth century. Very rare," the Professor exclaimed.

"To these Defenders of the Faith groupies, they seem like they are about a dime a dozen," Milt said as they left O'Brien's office.

Once outside, Rid said, "Any more doubts about Presterman being Dean Floyd?"

"None. We are walking right into his trap," Milt replied.

"That's the way I figure it. We better have a plan by the time we get to New York," Rid agreed as he pulled onto the south bound ramp of I-95, heading for the Big Apple. A light snow was beginning to fall.

THIRTY-NINE

New York City

Milt and Rid had alternated driving to New York. Due to the snow through most of New England, they arrived after midnight. They had called ahead to the Intercontinental for a room. The hotel was the Barclay in earlier times and it was the favorite of many British travelers. It was on 48th Street, between Park and Lexington Avenues. The lobby remained like the old hotel: very ornate, with a huge bird cage in the middle of the floor. Panels had been placed over the cage sides so the birds could sleep.

When Milt went to the desk to register, the clerk looked at his monitor and said, "Welcome back, Mr. Young. It's been some time since we've seen you."

"New line of work. Doesn't bring me to New York as much as my old job. I miss it."

"The reservation says you have a Mr. Taylor with you."

"Yes. He is putting the car in the garage across the street. He'll be right in," Milt replied.

"To welcome you back, we have a very nice two-bedroom suite you can have for the price of the two rooms you requested," the clerk offered.

"That will be fine. Nonsmoking?"

"Of course. Here are your keys. It's room 2001.

At that moment, Rid arrived. They had only flight bags on rollers, so they declined the bellman's offer to take their bags and went straight up to their room. They did call room service and ordered bottles of Beefeater gin and Dalmore single malt scotch to unwind after the snowy drive. They sipped their drinks and talked for about another hour about their approach to Johnathan Presterman.

Rid suggested, "Let me go in alone. I can tell him you are prepared to go to the authorities if I don't come back."

"That should work. Plus you can offer your services again like you did in his scheme to privatize the world's military," Milt grinned.

"It worked once. Who knows?" Rid shot back.

"What about a gun? Will you be carrying?" Milt went on.

"No. All these office buildings use metal detectors since the catastrophe at the World Trade Center. I'll be all right," Rid assured his partner.

"Take along one of our transmitters so I can listen," Milt said.

"I will. Now let's get some sleep. I want to call Ricardo in the morning to see how Liu is doing and if they have made any progress on the search for the original Prester John's treasure."

"Okay, Rid. Good night."

"Good night, Milt. See you around eight."

"Make it 8:30," Milt said as he went into his bedroom and closed the door.

FORTY

New York City

When Milt walked into the sitting room of the suite the next morning, there was a full room-service breakfast set on the coffee table. Ridley was at the desk on the phone. He covered the mouth piece and said, "It's Ricardo. Get on the extension in your room."

Milt grabbed a cup of tea and retreated to his bedroom. He picked up the phone and said, "Ricardo. How goes the search?"

"I was just getting ready to tell Rid. Liu is a terrific researcher. She has found another reference to a possible site for Prester John's palace."

"Where?" Rid asked.

"In Africa. Further south than we assumed he traveled. It's a place called the Great Zimbabwe. It's a huge area with plenty of water. It was inhabited by as many as 20,000 people for 400 years covering the time of the Presbyter's letter to Emperor Manuel I. Later the area was abandoned. Whoever they were, they simply disappeared. They were great builders, astronomers, and mathematicians."

"Sounds like the Mayans. Their civilization disappeared about the same time," Rid said.

"Or the Incas at Machu Picchu. Or the Nabateans at Petra. That's four advanced cultures that built great cities and places of worship, then completely disappeared without a trace. That would make an interesting study for one of my history experts," the Curator said. "Ah. Here comes Liu now." He waved to the young Chinese girl and said, "It's the travelers, Milt and Rid."

Liu picked up the phone on Ricardo's secretary's desk and excitedly said, "Did the Monsignor tell you the news?"

"Yes. He said you did a terrific job digging out a possible reference to Prester John being further south in Africa. What did they call the place?" Rid complimented Liu.

She replied, "It is called the Great Zimbabwe. A long-lost city in the country now called Zimbabwe in honor of the ancients who lived there."

"What's your feel for whether it could be the place we might find P.J.?" Milt ask for a conclusion.

"It's big enough, fancy enough, advanced in its design and construction, and has plenty of water. But it is awfully far south," she answered.

"I've never been there. It's near Botswana, right?" Rid wanted to know.

"Right next door. Their common border is, in part, the Zambezi River and the famous Victoria Falls," she replied.

"Put it on our list of places to visit," Rid changed the subject. "I am meeting with Johnathan Presterman, that is Dean Floyd, this afternoon. Milt and I are certain it's Floyd because dropping that name to his contact drew an immediate invitation. I'll add this Zimbabwe site to Beijing, Ethiopia, and the steppes and ask him to fund full archeological exploration of them all."

"Will he do that?" Ricardo asked.

"I doubt it. Although we checked his stock earlier and the EPIC corporation is doing quite well," Milt interjected.

"Good luck," Liu said. "Be careful. You say this man is dangerous."

"We've met before. We have a plan. We'll be okay," Rid assured her. "We need to go now to finalize the arrangements with an intermediary. An investment banker named Gold. Ciao!"

"Ciao!" Milt echoed.

Followed by Ricardo's, "Arrivederci."

Then Liu got in the spirit with her own, "Ciao, signori."

FORTY-ONE

New York City

Ridley Taylor called Samuel Gold at 10:30. The automated voicemail answering system said, "Thank you for calling Richards and Clark. Your call is important to us, so please listen to the following options. If you know the extension number of the person you are calling, you may dial it at any time. If you are checking your accounts, press one. If you are inquiring about one of our stock recommendations, press two. If you want to set up a new account, press three. If you want to buy or sell securities, press four. If you want to speak to a customer service representative, press zero."

Rid pushed the zero button and heard, "Thank you for calling Richards and Clark. All of our customer service representatives are busy. Please stay on the line as your call is very important to us."

With that, Rid began to listen to elevator music interspersed with short messages. The messages kept assuring Rid his call was important and that it may be monitored for training purposes. After three "importants" and two "trainings" a real person said, "This is Norma. How may I direct your call?"

"Give me Samuel Gold's office."

Gold's secretary answered on the first ring, "Mr. Gold's office. May I help you?"

"I sure hope so. It's taken me twenty minutes to get to you. My name is Ridley Taylor. I was to call Mr. Gold to set up a meeting with his client, Johnathan Presterman."

"Oh, yes. Mr. Gold told me you would be calling. He is in a meeting, but I am to page him to tell him you are on the line. I'll put you on hold. It should only be a moment before he will answer."

This time there was only elevator music. *Claire d' Lune* was just starting when Rid heard, "Sam Gold here, Mr. Taylor. Thank you for calling."

"Thank you for being there. Have you set a meeting with Presterman?"

"Yes. He ask that you and Mr. Young meet with him at two this afternoon in one of our conference rooms. It's room number 6019 on the sixtieth floor."

"What's the address?" Rid needed to know.

"We are at 224 Park Avenue. That's the northeast corner of Park Avenue and 46th Street. I'll arrange for your two guest badges to be at our security desk in the lobby."

"I may only need one badge. My partner has some other work to do."

"I'll leave two in case he does come. May I help in any other way?" Gold said as he prepared to hang up.

"No. Thank you for your help." Rid then turned to Milt who had been listening on their parlor extension and said, "Don't you hate voicemail?"

"It's the pits," Milt agreed. "But their building is only two blocks down the street."

"That's the old American Brands Building. I visited there one time when I was working on a tobacco-related case. Let's get rid of the car and have some lunch."

Then they discussed their plan for the afternoon. Both of them would enter the building and get their guest badges. Rid would go on up to the meeting room. Milt would wait five minutes, and then go up to the sixtieth floor and stay in the men's room. He should be able to listen to Rid's transmitter from there.

Just before two, they arrived at the skyscraper headquarters of R&B. The lobby directory listed the firm as occupying the top seven floors of the sixty-one-story building. As they looked at the directory's list of other tenants, they saw that EPIC had space on floors seventeen through nineteen.

"Doesn't look like Presterman will have far to go to make our meeting," Rid quipped.

"Wonder why he didn't meet us in his office?" Milt asked.

"Afraid we might tell his employees who he really is," suggested Rid.

"Could be. You better go on up. It's almost two."

Rid stepped into the half-full express elevator to floors fifty to sixty. He was aware of the two strong-arm types standing on either side of him. The elevator dropped off people on fifty-two, fifty-three, fifty-six, and fifty-eight. When it reached the sixtieth, only Rid and his two guides were left.

They walked out of the elevator car and one of them said, "This way."

Then they forced him across the foyer and onto a local elevator being held by a third ox-like man. They descended to the seventeenth floor. There they escorted him to the end of the hall to an executive conference room with a table large enough to seat twenty people. There was a huge electrified map of the world at one end with live current buzzing across its face. No one was there. The two pulled out guns and told Rid they wanted to search him.

"I'm not carrying a weapon. How did you get those in here?" Rid said as he spread his arms.

"We ship them in as freight. We're licensed to have them as part of EPIC's security force. Your safe. We just wanted to make certain you were clean. Now, just wait here. We'll be right outside, if you need us."

As they left the room, another door at the end of the room opened and a man entered. "I'm Roy Posner. Mr. Taylor, right?"

"Right. Where is Presterman?" Rid demanded.

"He was called on a conference call with our team in Russia who are trying to finalize our take over of that country's electric generating facilities. He has to be on the phone to finish the deal."

"What do we do now?" Rid was visibly angry.

"He sent me to get started with you. He will be here when the call is over. I am Presterman's chief of staff. I know everything about our operations and I and Professor O'Brien are the only ones who are familiar with your search for Prester John's treasure."

"Okay. Here's the deal. These pictures were taken outside Beijing, China, at a site Marco Polo believed was the palace of Prester John. Look at the outlines of the Christian fish. We think this mosaic floor was a map of the Prester's kingdoms. Note the larger fish. Maybe the locations of his vast treasure. To continue our search, we need large sums of money to finance explorations."

"I see. And what about your partner? Where is he?" Posner asked.

Before Rid could answer, the main door opened and Milt entered at gunpoint followed by the previous guards and a third one that had not been in the elevator. That guard was holding Milt's listening device. "Where's your transmitter?" he said to Rid.

"My lapel pin. I don't need it now," Rid said.

The door at the end of the room opened and Dean Floyd, alias Johnathan Presterman, walked in. "So, Misters Taylor and Young, we meet again. I hope our discussions are more friendly this time." He held up his hand to stop the two from speaking. Then he asked the guards to step outside, leaving only Roy Posner, who also had a gun. "I've been listening on the intercom system. Let me see these pictures." He studied them for several minutes, then said, "This truly is a remarkable discovery. It verifies what my grandfather, father, and I have thought for many years. Prester John was real. I knew you were the right people to find him."

"We don't have him yet," Rid said. "Before we continue we are concerned about a personal problem you left in England."

"I am now a citizen of Brazil. They have no extradition agreement with Great Britain," he answered.

"What about your new scheme? This EPIC thing?" Milt asked.

"A perfectly legal, tax-paying conglomerate that specializes in acquiring weak electric companies. Everything here is subject to review by the Securities and Exchange Commission, the many power industry regulators, the Federal Trade Commission, the IRS, and our own external auditors. This is a completely legitimate, above-board business enterprise that is enjoying rapid growth and success. Now, what are your intentions?" Floyd peered over his half reading glasses at the two visitors.

"We could tell you we want to continue the search," Rid began. "There is a great pile of money to be made."

"I trusted you once before about your working for me. I'll not repeat that mistake. Again, what are your intentions?"

Milt responded, "We could expose you, and your electric empire will collapse. And you are not in Brazil now. I believe the United States does extradite to England."

"Those are things I would expect you to do," Presterman said as he pushed a button under the table. "But I think we are no longer in need of your services."

The three guards reentered the room.

"Take these two down to the first-aid room. Hold them there," he ordered.

As they were being escorted out of the room, they heard Floyd say to Posner, "Call the retreat on Long Island and tell them to get ready for visitors. Also get the helicopter to land on the roof."

After a short wait in the first-aid room, Presterman and a diminutive nurse with a very evil smile walked in. She said, "I've been waiting a long time for this. I am the daughter of Franz Schwarz, who you killed in England."

"Not us," Milt said as he pointed to Floyd. "Him."

"He told me what happened. I blame you." She turned to the guards and said for them to hold the two men still. Then she took two hypodermic needles out of a cabinet and stuck one in each of the heroes. They were not even awake long enough to hear Presterman tell the guards to put them on the gurneys in the clinic room and take them to the roof. Nor did they hear the roar of the helicopters engines as it took off for an unknown retreat somewhere on Long Island.

FORTY-TWO

Long Island

Ridley was drowning in a sea of black, swampy water. He was clawing his way toward the light at the surface, but his lungs were about to burst. His head was pounding . . . pounding . . . he started to shake. Then his eyes fought the stickiness and he tried to open them. As he started to come out of his drug-induced stupor, he shook his head and shivered. Then he began to realize he wasn't in water at all. He slowly began to take in his surroundings. He was lying on an unmade bed in a very luxurious bedroom. He could see Milt on the next twin bed dressed only in his boxer shorts. He was out cold. Rid felt his own body to discover that he too wore only his jockey shorts. He was cold.

Rid tried to rise but fell back. On his third attempt he was able to hang his legs over the side of the bed and finally he sat up. The pain in his head was almost unbearable. He tried to remember what had happened to the two of them. He remembered the confrontation with Dean Floyd in New York. And then the daughter of Franz Schwarz coming into a room. He could visualize the hypodermic needle. "That's it!" he thought to himself. "We've been drugged."

He tried to stand. He fell on his knees. He crawled to Milt's bed and shook him to no avail. Then he pulled himself to his feet and stumbled across the room to the window. He pulled back the heavy drape and the bright sunlight temporarily blinded him. He saw there were bars on the window. He looked out across a long expanse of well-manicured lawn and landscaping. He could see a high brick wall and over that the sea. He surmised they were in Dean's, or Presterman's, mansion that must be near New York. Perhaps the Connecticut shore, or eastern Long Island. But how did they get here? And how long had he been out? He heard Milt start to groan. He went back to his own bed and sat on the edge and watched as Milt echoed his own return from the drug world.

When Milt opened his eyes, Rid said, "Welcome to somewhere where the sun is shining and there is a beautiful sea for swimming. All we have to do is get through the bars on the windows."

"How about the door?" Milt moaned.

"Haven't tried to walk that far. I just woke up a few minutes ago."

"Any thoughts on where we are?" Milt began to plan their escape.

"Big estate somewhere near New York. Dean's executive retreat, no doubt," Rid replied.

"Help me up, Rid. Hey! I don't have any clothes on," Milt discovered.

"You should have worn your Joe Boxers with the happy face," Rid joked.

"I'm not ready for your humor yet. Let's figure out how to get out of here."

At that moment they heard a key in the door. It opened and the nurse with two guards entered.

"You sounded pretty happy on our monitor a moment ago, so I thought I would change your mood. Do you remember me?" the nurse asked.

"I remember the evil smile," Rid said. "I woke up with that image."

"I saw you, too. You were in New York," Milt added. "You're the one who drugged us!"

"Very good. Yes, we met very briefly in New York two days ago. I am Sascha Schwarz. Daughter of the man you murdered in England."

"We told you, it was Floyd, or Presterman, who killed your father," Milt interrupted.

"It was you who started the gun battle. Who tried to interfere with Sir Dean's plans for a new world order. I blame you. And now I will have my revenge," she shouted. She turned to the two guards and ordered, "Bring them to my laboratory." Then she turned and marched out of the room.

"Let's go!" the guards said waving their guns toward the door.

"How about clothes?" Rid asked.

"And where is Presterman?" Milt wanted to know.

"No clothes. Presterman's not here. Now, get moving."

They were ushered down a long hall to an elevator that took them down three floors to a finished lower level. They walked through a large game room that opened onto a large patio and swimming pool area. Then down a hall and into a windowless room that looked like a mad scientist's lab. Both had thoughts of what their fate might be at the hands of such a small but evil woman.

FORTY-THREE

Long Island

The room had two surgical tables on one side, a tiled wall on the other with a fire hose, and two chairs that looked like those used for electrocutions in the middle.

"Strap them in the chairs," Nurse Schwarz commanded. The guards obeyed.

"I still think you should let us talk to Presterman. We can help him," Milt implored.

"Yes," Rid continued. "He didn't even hear our proposal. We know we can deliver Prester John's treasure. But not if we are dead."

"Dead is what you will be, after I find out all you know about the treasure. And who else knows Johnathan's true identity," she smirked.

"No one else knows as much as the two of us. You won't get it out of us either," Rid said confidently.

"We will see," she replied as she pulled Rid's jockey shorts aside and attached an electrode to his scrotum. "We will see." She went to the control box and turned a dial slowly. Rid could feel small electrical vibrations enter his body. He tensed and began to recite

Hiawatha to himself to ignore the pain. Then she twisted the dial rapidly, and Rid's body lurched. He screamed with pain and passed out, slumping in the chair.

"We'll get you for this!" Milt yelled.

I don't think so," she said calmly. "Now it's your turn, unless you want to tell me what I want to know."

"I'll tell you, I'm not the hero Taylor tries to be. Besides, there isn't that much that you don't already know."

"I'll give you one chance," she said as she turned on a tape recorder.

Milt was careful to give them a complete account of all the information he figured they already knew, plus he made up a story about how they planned to find the seventy-two locations on Prester John's map using the facilities of the Sun Yat Sen University in Beijing and satellite imaging from the U.S. space program. He minimized how much others like Monsignor Corso and Liu Chow Lim knew; he left others, like the Keenes, Byerlies, and Countess Von Anton, out entirely. He talked for about twenty minutes, trying to make it sound convincing. When he finished, he said, "Play this tape for Mr. Presterman. I'm sure he'll change his mind."

"I'll play it for him. How do you have access to the satellite imaging?" she wanted to know.

"Taylor still has connections through the CIA. We've used it before. That's something Presterman needs us for."

"He will very much want all this information. It may even be useful at his annual shareholders meeting next week. Thank you for being so forthcoming. But, for my father, I will give you a dose of my electric revenge anyway," she said as she attached the electrodes.

Later, when both Young and Taylor had returned to consciousness back in their bedroom, they found they were dressed like people going fishing.

"We still have time, Rid. Nurse Evil told me the shareholder meeting is next week."

"That means we haven't been here for more than a couple of days," Rid calculated.

The door opened and the two goons with guns came in.

"Come on, we're going for a boat ride," one said as he tossed each of them a pair of handcuffs. "Here put these on."

They were led down to the boat house where a thirty-two-foot Sea Ray with twin Mercury 150-horsepower engines was tied to the dock. They were shoved aboard and pushed past a small rubber dinghy into the cabin. They heard the engines roar to life and pull away. Soon they were going full speed across a bay they could see out the side windows.

"I've been here before," Rid said. "This looks like the Shinnecock Bay off West Hampton, Long Island. Yes, there is the inlet to the Atlantic and Tana Beach."

One of the gunmen entered the cabin. "Quiet," he said.

"Where are we going?" Milt asked,

"Where you're going doesn't matter. Cause you ain't comin back," he snickered.

"What?" Rid cried.

"You two fishermen are going to have an accident. That's all you need to know. Now keep it quiet," he said as he went back on deck.

The two stayed quiet but searched the cabin. Milt found some map pins on the navigation chart table. Using one he quickly removed his handcuffs and then those of Taylor. "Learned that in your school at Quantico," he whispered. They returned to their seats and pretended to have the cuffs attached. After about twenty minutes cruising straight out into the Atlantic, they heard the engines shut down. "This is it," Rid mouthed, "Be ready."

One of the guards entered waving his gun and said, "Okay. On deck."

The boat was rocking in the waves. The other guard was pushing the dinghy over the side. It was tied to the stern.

The first guard said, "Pick up those fishing poles. Then I'm going to remove your cuffs and we are going to leave you two to enjoy the rest of your day."

"You mean the rest of their lives," the other laughed.

"I don't know how to fish," Milt shrugged. "Which end do you hold?"

The second guard approached him to put the pole in his hands. The boat lurched in a wave. Rid and Milt jumped the two guards, knocking their guns aside and pushed them to the deck. Milt retrieved one of the guns and motioned the two former captors to the seat at the stem.

"Now, what's about to happen on this boat?" Rid asked.

"It's going to blow. And soon. I set the timer for only five minutes," one of them screamed.

"Then goodbye," the heroes said as they dove for the dinghy.

"Don't leave us!" one of them started to say as the boat exploded in a fireball that threw Milt and Rid fifteen yards out into the ocean.

The wreckage rained down on the Janus pair, who ducked several objects by going under water. When the firestorm was over, there was debris everywhere but no sign of the goons. Rid found one of the pontoons from the dinghy and clung to it while he swam over to Milt. They both hung on and tried to talk, but neither of them could hear.

After about fifteen minutes the ringing in their ears began to fade. Milt said, "That was close."

"Too close," Rid agreed. "Now we owe Johnathan Presterman slash Dean Floyd twice over."

"It's time we paid him another visit," Milt agreed.

"Maybe we can go to his shareholder meeting," Rid suggested.

"That could be fun," Milt laughed.

They heard another boat in the distance. A few minutes later an older Aquasport center console fishing boat came up and the two local sportsmen pulled Rid and Milt aboard.

"What the hell happened?" one of them asked in a real Long Island accent.

"Yeah, we heard the blast and saw the fireball from near the beach," the bigger one said.

"Wish we knew," Rid replied. "We were guests on the boat. The two guides must have been killed in the explosion."

"We were fishing off the back, and luckily were thrown clear," Milt added. "We sure are glad you saw it and came to pick us up. Thanks!"

"Yeah. There are sharks out here. With all the cuts you two have, they would have found you soon enough. Pete, get the first-aid kit. That's Pete Voss. I'm John Seh. We're both from the North Fork around Aquebogue and Mattituck."

"I'm Milt Young from England and this is my American friend from the city, Ridley Taylor. Where can you take us?"

"There is a Coast Guard station at Hampton Bays, just inside the inlet," the one named Voss said as he returned with the first-aid kit.

"That would be good," Rid said. "I'm sure they picked up the blast on their monitors and will want a report."

As the boat made its way back toward the inlet they were passed by a helicopter heading out to the site of the wreckage. Milt and Rid began to formulate their story for the authorities.

FORTY-FOUR

Long Island

When the two fishermen, John and Pete, dropped Rid and Milt off at the Coast Guard station at Hampton Bays, there was a welcoming committee on the dock. Lieutenant Commander Lois Lester and Suffolk County Deputy Sheriff Wilfred Grathwohl led the two inside, eager to hear about the explosion.

"We will tell you all we can, but it involves national security," Rid began once they were in the office. "I'm Ridley Taylor and this is Milt Young. We don't have our credentials, but we are connected to the CIA. If you will permit me to use your phone, I think we can clear this up very quickly."

Commander Lester handed the phone to Taylor. He dialed the field access number and gave his code. "Connect me to Deputy Director Bryan Robert," he said.

Almost immediately, Bryan came on the phone, saying, "Where the hell have you two been the last three days? I've had a whole team looking for you since you didn't return from Presterman's office."

"Hold on, Bryan. We'll fill you in on all of that later. Right now I am sitting in the station chief's office at the Coast Guard station at Hampton Bays, Long Island. The Chief is Lieutenant Commander Lois Lester. Milt and I were on a boat that blew up off the coast about an hour ago. It is part of our current assignment. Will you vouch for us?"

Rid handed the phone to the Commander. She listened intently for a few moments and then said, "I understand. Yes. I will call back for verification."

She hung up and said, "This matter is, as you say, a matter of national security. You may tell us whatever you are willing to release. Then I am to call Deputy Robert back at the CIA's published number."

"We were being held prisoner at an estate near here. I can't give you the name," Rid explained. "The boating accident was intended to get rid of us, but we were able to turn the tables on our captors. We don't know the names of the two you may find among the wreckage. And I can't give you the name of their employer."

"We can probably determine that ourselves from the boat registration," the Deputy Sheriff said.

"Perhaps," Milt cautioned. "But you may not release any details or approach the owner without clearance from the agency."

"All right. That's enough for us. Let me make that return call," Lester said. She dialed the phone and was patched through to Bryan Robert without delay. Again, she listened intently, and said "Yes sir," as she handed the phone to Ridley.

"What next, Bryan?" he asked.

"A helicopter is on its way to you now, ETA six or seven minutes," Robert said.

"That quick?" Rid was surprised.

"It's coming from the old Grumman Aircraft factory in Calverton. We still test fighter planes there. It's only about twenty miles from your location."

"What then?" Rid went on.

"I'll take the agency's Citation and be there within the hour. Then we can plan our next moves," Bryan said.

As Rid returned the phone to its cradle, the rotors of the helicopter could be heard making their approach to the Coast Guard station's heli-pad.

"Thank you for your understanding," Milt said to the two officials as he and Rid went outside to board the chopper.

"This will probably become more clear in just a few days," Rid said, "We will tell you more when we can."

As the helicopter was lifting off, Milt leaned over to Rid and said, "I wish I knew what we are going to be able to tell those two in a few days. But I'm not sure how this thing is going to play out."

"Not to worry, partner. Old Rid has a plan."

FORTY-FIVE

Calverton, Long Island

Milt and Rid waited in an office next to the large hangar where the National Transportation and Safety Board had been restoring the wreckage of TWA Flight 800, which had exploded a few years before near the site of their boat explosion. The huge partial plane looked eerie in the semi-dark hangar.

"Seems like we're going to spend the day around exploded vehicles," Rid said.

"Yeah," Milt replied. "We fared better than the poor souls on that one. Now, what's your plan?"

"I'm working on it. Wait till Bryan gets here," Rid pleaded.

"Just like I thought. Another famous Taylor 'make it up as you go' plan," Milt chided.

"I do have an idea, Milt. It's just a little bizarre. Now, let me think it through."

Thirty-five minutes later, Bryan Robert's CIA plane landed at the base, and he joined the other two in the office. "So, what happened?" he opened.

"Not much to tell," Rid replied. "We were drugged and kidnapped to Presterman's private estate on the South Shore."

"Tortured, too!" Milt interjected. "By no less an evil person than the daughter of Franz Schwarz."

"The mean guy that was with Floyd in England?" Bryan asked.

"The same," Rid verified. "We both will be singing a couple of octaves higher after her electric entertainment."

"That doesn't sound like fun. Can you show me this place?" Bryan wanted to know.

"From the sea side, we can," Rid stated. "But Presterman isn't there. "They said he was in New York, getting ready for the EPIC shareholder meeting."

"Will the people out here know you escaped?" Robert went on.

"Not if the news says four people were killed in the explosion," Milt suggested.

"Good idea!" Bryan agreed. "That way Presterman will think he is rid of you."

"Precisely my idea," Rid interrupted. "You must have been reading my mind. Milt, I think we wait until his big day and then show up at his stockholder meeting. He is still wanted on an open warrant for treason in England. We could arrest him in front of the crowd and have precleared extradition papers for us to escort him to London."

"Sounds good. We'll find out where and when the meeting will be, and we'll keep the estate out here under surveillance," Robert concurred. "Now, Milt, you get hold of Jeremy Watson at MI6 and tell him of our plan. He may want to come over for the meeting. I'll get the extradition papers in Washington. Then let's meet in New York tomorrow to finalize the plan."

"Should we stay somewhere other than the Intercontinental?" Milt asked.

"It may be watched by either Presterman or our friends from the Defenders of the Faith of Prester John."

"We'll use our safehouse on East 71st Street. You know it, Rid?" Bryan suggested.

"I know it."

"I'll have the helicopter take you in. You can fly over and identify the estate on your way. I'll take the Citation and return to Washington. Need anything else?" Bryan started to leave.

"Clothes," Rid replied.

"And money," Milt added.

"And guns, and food, and a very stiff drink," Rid completed the list.

"Just tell them at the safehouse. See you tomorrow," Bryan said as he walked out of the office.

One of the helicopter pilots came to get them about five minutes later. As they were walking out of the hangar, Milt turned to Rid and said, "You really are crazy. We're going to just walk into a meeting of several hundred people and arrest the speaker?"

"Not walk in, my friend. Swagger. I'm going to enjoy this," Rid replied as he stepped up into the chopper.

FORTY-SIX

New York City

After locating Presterman's estate near Westhampton for the helicopter crew, the chopper turned west and flew them the eighty-mile length of Long Island to the New York Port Authority's East River Heliport. A CIA staff car was waiting there to take Milt and Rid to the safehouse on the Upper East Side. The field agent at the desk that day was known to Ridley Taylor.

"Fitz!" he exclaimed, "What are you doing here in New York?"

John Fitzgerald had replaced Taylor as the chief of station in Bern, Switzerland, several years earlier. "When I left Bern, I didn't retire from the Firm to make a bundle of money like you. But it was time for an old hand like me to man a desk. And this is a good one. With all the United Nations intrigue swirling around this city, it's the best of both worlds. A desk job with enough field work to keep me excited."

"Sounds ideal, Fitz. But where did you get the idea we're making bundles?" Milt interjected.

"The stories about you two are becoming the new legend of the agency. Your Faust affair and the finding of a Third Crusade treasure chest are major water cooler conversation pieces," Fitzgerald retorted. "But I've been told you are here on official business. How can I help?"

"Here's a list of things we need I wrote down on the way in," Rid handed Fitz a piece of paper. "We also want to get hold of a proxy statement for the shareholder meeting of EPIC. And we'll need some kind of credentials to get us in their meeting, We understand it is the day after tomorrow.."

Milt added, "I need a safe line to call Jeremy Watson at MI6."

"We have a direct, scrambled connection in the communications room downstairs. But first, let me show you your rooms. And I'll get started on your list. I see you've listed your clothing sizes," Fitzgerald commented.

"Actually, first," Rid said. "We were nearly beaten, shot, blown up, and drowned this morning. What I want first is a big glass of Dewar's scotch on the rocks. "

"Bombay gin, neat, for me," Milt added eagerly.

"I'll have the steward bring the drinks to your rooms. You can tell him what you want for dinner. I assume you plan to dine here," Fit replied.

"Right. We've got to work on our plan," Ridley began. "Did Bryan say when he'd be here?"

"He said he would pick up some deportation papers you need tomorrow morning and, then, he plans to be here by two in the afternoon. Will that work?"

"Sounds good," Milt said. "That should give Jeremy time to get here and to have British transportation ready for our quarry."

Rid and Milt went to their rooms, downed their drinks, showered, and lay down to rest. Within an hour, their requested clothes, money, and weapons were delivered, along with proxy statements for the upcoming shareholder meeting of EPIC.

Then Fitzgerald got them together in Rid's room to ask about the type of credentials they thought would work best.

"How about some from the financial press?" Rid suggested.

"Great idea!" chimed in Milt. "It worked the last time we crashed one of Dean Floyd's Meetings. I think I worked for the U.K.'s *Economist.*"

"I like the irony," Rid started. "Was I with the *Wall Street Journal*?"

"Nothing so high-powered," Milt joked, "It was more like *The Bear Market Bulletin.*"

"Very funny. This time, I believe I want to be high-profile so let's make it the *Journal.*"

"I'll get on it," Fitz said as he left the two together.

"I'm getting excited about this scheme of yours, Rid," Milt said with a salute.

"Were finally going to beard our lion in his den," Rid smiled as he returned the gesture. "See you at dinner about seven."

"Maybe with another round of drinks first," Milt suggested.

"At least one, my friend. At least one!"

FORTY-SEVEN

New York City

The two former spies were both excited when they met for breakfast in the CIA safehouse dining room early the next morning. They had each found their requested press credentials and passes to the EPIC shareholder meeting slipped under their bedroom doors. Along with the passes they found new identity papers. Milt Young was posing as Lynn Merritt, an actual senior reporter for the *Economist.* Ridley Taylor carried the ID of a *Wall Street Journal* business analyst, Bill Martin, whose specialty was the electric utility industry.

"I've been promoted to senior reporter status," Milt said as they sat down to a full breakfast of Western omelets with sausage, biscuits, and orange juice. Milt had English breakfast tea at his place and Rid had caffe latte, which he had gained the taste for since living in Rome.

"And I, sir, have been covering EPIC for the last two years for the *Journal.*" Rid quickly changed the subject. "How did they know I now drink caffe latte in the mornings?"

"This is the CIA, Rid. And Fitz said yesterday everyone at the agency was interested in our second careers," Milt replied.

"Yeah, it's easy to forget how we former spooks knew everything about everyone. So," Rid mumbled through a full bite of the omelet, "Bryan won't be here until two. What do we do this morning?"

"Jeremy called me back early this morning to say that he and a recovery team would be landing in an RAF jet at Tetoboro Airport in New Jersey at 9:30 this morning. He should be here before eleven," Milt answered.

"Good. We can meet with him to plan the extraction and departure of Mr. Presterman, a.k.a. Dean. Tetoboro is a relatively quiet place for private and corporate aircraft. I hope they're not coming in a military plane."

"No. I'm sure they'll be in one the government uses. It only carries the British diplomatic markings," Milt said.

"That shouldn't be too conspicuous. Okay, we'll plan to meet with Jeremy at eleven. In the mean time, I'm going to call Ricardo at the Vatican and tell him we are back in action. I also want to see how he and Liu are doing on their search for the original Prester John and his treasure," Rid explained.

"I'm going to have another pot of this excellent English tea. You go ahead. I'll set up the conference room with Fitzgerald for our meetings at eleven and two," Milt said as he lifted his cup as if in a toast.

Rid smiled and headed to the communications room. There he got on a secure line and phoned Monsignor Corso in his private office at the Vatican.

A strong voice answered, "Bon giorno! This is Father Corso."

"Ricardo, it's Ridley Taylor."

"It's three o'clock in the afternoon. We've been waiting to hear from you. Are you all right? We haven't heard from you for several days," the Priest was eager to hear the details of his friends' activities.

"It's a long story. Presterman kidnapped us, flew us to his private estate on Long Island, had us tortured, and tried to blow us up on a boat. But both Milt and I are safe. We are in New York City, where we will take Presterman, or Dean Floyd if you prefer, into custody tomorrow. The British and U.S. governments are working together on a plan to quickly extradite him back to England to stand trial on the old treason charges."

"Sounds like you have been busy. I'm glad you are safe. We have good news as well," Corso countered.

"That's really why I called. How goes the search?" Rid asked.

"Liu continues to do an excellent job. She has eliminated the Great Zimbabwe as a possibility. Other research on that site confirm it was an advanced culture of African origin. Her research on the conquests of Genghis Khan strongly suggest that Marco Polo was right. We now believe Khan ransacked the Prester's treasure and used it to finance his own expedition into the Middle East and Europe. If there is any treasure left, Liu believes it would either be in Samarkand, where the Khan had his last encampment or back in Mongolia in his tomb; which, as you know, has never been found. In fact there is a current expedition financed and led by some insurance man from Chicago trying to get permission to look for the Khan's burial site."

"I remember reading something about that in the *USA Today* recently. Are they searching?" Rid was eager to know.

"We haven't got that far, but we will be working on that this afternoon," the Monsignor said.

"I'll let you go. Say hello to Liu for me," Rid said. "You said you had good news? Maybe the two of you can call me back later today. I can be reached here all day."

"I promised Liu I would let her tell you. We'll call you later," Ricardo replied.

He gave the Curator the number and then hung up the phone, thinking about how he missed being with Liu. He wondered if she felt the same.

FORTY-EIGHT

New York City

The rest of the day was very busy for Milt and Rid. Their meeting with Jeremy and the British extraction team came first. Jeremy was accompanied by two other field officers from MI6 and three commandos dressed in Savile Row suits.

"Besides the six of us," Jeremy began, "we have a crew of four operating the jet, two senior officers from Scotland Yard, and a bailiff to take Sir Dean into custody once we have him in the air and therefore on our 'soil,' so to speak."

"Good work, Jeremy," Ridley replied, "Bryan will be here at two this afternoon and he will fill us in on the U.S. ground team that will escort him to the Tetoboro Airport."

Ridley went on to describe how he and Milt planned to enter the shareholder meeting and confront Floyd/Presterman in front of the crowd. They would cover all the exits from the ballroom as well as all doors to the hotel.

"Which hotel will have the meeting?" one of the other agents asked.

"The Waldorf Astoria," Milt answered. "Perhaps the most luxurious in the city, and very British, too. The main lobby centerpiece is a clock that was given to the owner by Queen Victoria herself after a stay there."

The English team all nodded their collective approval.

"After our meeting with Mr. Robert, could we tour the hotel to see the layout?" a commando asked.

"That is an excellent suggestion. Milt and I probably shouldn't be seen there, as EPIC will have their security staff there in advance of the meeting," Rid answered.

"Let's assume also," Milt added, "that Dean and his technical people might be there rehearsing. These shareholder meetings can be quite large productions."

"On second thought, I say we don't tour the hotel," Jeremy decided. "I'm sure Bryan can get us floor plans and any other info we need from the local authorities."

"Correct decision," Rid agreed. "You fellows must be tired after flying most of the night. Let me have our host, John Fitzgerald, fix you up with quarters where you can rest and clean up. I'll have them fix some lunch for all of us at one o'clock. Then Bryan should be here and we can finish our planning,"

"How about that!" the other commando said, "They even got us an Irish host."

With that, they all were shown to shared rooms for two in the safehouse. Rid called Bryan to tell him about the meeting and to suggest he get a floor plan of the hotel.

"Already have it, Rid. New York's Deputy Chief of Police, Don Barnes, is a good friend of mine. We played basketball against each other in college. He'll bring the plans to our two o'clock meeting."

"Thanks, you're out in front of us as usual. Do you have the rest of the needed paperwork?"

"I'm on my way over to the State Department right now to pick them up. Then straight out to Andrews to hop the plane to New York," Bryan said.

"You may want to land at Tetoboro in New Jersey. That's where the Brits have their plane," Rid suggested.

"Tetoboro it is. See you at two," Bryan said as he hung up the phone.

Lunch was a choice of English beef and kidney pie or fried chicken. The entire British team chose the chicken. Lunch was ending about 1:50 when Bryan and several others entered the room.

"Let's get to work," he said. Everyone followed him to the conference room. Once there, he introduced Deputy Chief Barnes of the New York Police, lead FBI Agent for New York, Bob Lawley, along with two of his agents, Anne Ramsey and Joe Victor. He finished the introductions with, "Milt I'm sure you and Rid remember Cathy Padget from our firm."

"Hi Cathy. Good to see you again," Milt said.

"Yeah, Cath. Ditto," added Rid. "Is this everyone?"

"Oh no. This is just the leadership. Each of us have as many resources available as we determine we need. And Chief Barnes has over a hundred police officers ready to block the streets for our motorcade," Bryan stated.

The meeting continued with a thorough review of the hotel layout. There were seven entrances to the Waldorf's main ballroom on the second and third floors, counting those from the foyers on two sides of the main floor, plus those on the balcony that ringed three of the sides of the two-story walls. There also were six doors from the kitchen, and two behind the stage that led to dressing rooms for performers. Finally there was a small door that led into the third-floor elevator foyer on the Park Avenue side.

"The head of the hotel's security staff tells me," Don Barnes began, "that this is the entrance and exit that Presterman and his board of directors and staff will use. They all have suites in the towers up those elevators. It takes a special ID and lapel pin to get through that door. And EPIC's own security insist that they man that station. So that is a soft spot for us to have direct control."

Anne Ramsey offered, "I could get some of our female agents to pose with me as the maid staff cleaning the rooms on that floor."

"Plan on it, Anne," Lead Agent Bob Lawley said.

"I'd like to provide one of our officers to be there too so you have local authority," Barnes insisted.

"Okay by me," Anne said.

"Me, too," added Lawley.

"Now, Rid, please tell us all about your grand plan to confront Presterman," Bryan passed the ball to Taylor.

Rid went on to describe how he and Milt were going to attend the meeting on press credentials, "We have read the meeting's proxy statement. It outlines the order of business. After the call to order and reading of the previous year's minutes, the first thing is a vote for members of the board of directors.

"While the vote tellers are counting any ballots submitted at the meeting along with the proxies that had been previously submitted, the Chairman will speak about the company's progress and future. He will probably use slides, video, and other media to enhance his presentation. If the room darkens during this, I plan to move closer to the stage, where Floyd will be able to see me when I stand. After his presentation, a report from the tellers will confirm the election of the directors. Then there will be a period where he and his staff will take questions from the floor. I will choose an appropriate time to address my question to the Chair. I plan to simply ask him if he isn't really Dean Floyd who is wanted for treason in England. After that, almost anything can happen. We have to remember the room is full of honest, innocent people. In fact, most of his board and staff are also innocent, so no shooting. We want to force him to run. If I can nab him, I will. If he comes through any of the other doors, have your personnel ready when the shouting begins. If, as it sounds like it may be, he uses the third-floor private door, I would have someone riding each of the elevators and in the stairwells. Agent Ramsey and her team can charge the door and secure Dean's private army. Remember, they probably will be armed. And when the room is dark Milt can move up to be close to the inside of that door. Finally, if he gets past any of the exits, I want everyone on the team to have communications so they can follow what's happening. That way, personnel at the hotel entrances will know if he is coining their way."

"Sounds, rather dramatic and dangerous," Chief Barnes warned. "I don't want any big gun battles in my city. Why don't we just go now and arrest him?"

"He'll have more firepower around him now, than he will on that stage. With the exception of the limited team of professional gunmen he'll have at that third-floor entrance, everyone else in the ballroom, including us, will have gone through metal detectors."

"Then, I want to alter your plan slightly," Bryan said. "After the meeting begins we'll have the elevator and stairwell agents join Anne and her team on a prearranged signal to neutralize his security force in the third-floor foyer."

"That's all right as long as they can do it quietly, so I don't lose the chance to confront this bastard. He has been Milt's and my enemy for over three years and he has had us shot at, bombed, drugged, and tortured on more than one occasion. I want to see the recognition in his face that his bid for world domination is as dead as he will be after his trial for treason."

"Okay, is everyone agreed?" Bryan asked as he looked around the huge table.

Each, in turn, nodded or spoke their assent. The meeting adjourned with agreement to meet at the Lexington Avenue entrance to the hotel at 9:45 the next morning. The meeting was to start at ten sharp.

When Ridley returned to his room their was an e-mail message that had come over the safehouse's secure system from Liu in Rome.

She said she was very excited to tell her friend Ridley that she had been granted amnesty by the Chinese government and that she could return to Beijing to work as Dr. Wu Ling's assistant in a new dig at the suspected site of Prester John's Palace. A dig that was being well financed by the Vatican. She went on to say that she hoped to see her friends Ridley and Milt before she left Rome in three days. Rid printed and then folded the message and put it in his pocket to show Milt. He wasn't sure if he could get to Rome in three days. As he continued to think about her, he became sure that he did not want to try to talk her out of going back to China. It was her home and the chance to help find the truth about Prester John was her life's ambition. Something inside him said, "Let her go, Rid."

FORTY-NINE

New York City

During cocktails before dinner at the safehouse, Ridley showed the message to Milt.

"Did you call or e-mail her back?" the reader wanted to know.

"Not yet. I'm trying to decide what to say," Rid answered.

"Are you going to try to get Liu to stay in Rome?" Milt asked, somewhat incredulously.

"No. I have decided she belongs in China doing her desired life's work. I just am looking for the words to express my feelings," Rid replied.

"Words of romance might confuse her," Milt volunteered.

"That's pretty much the conclusion I've reached. I think I'll just e-mail her back our good wishes and tell her we want to keep in touch about her findings on Prester John, in case she finds any clues about a treasure. That sound okay to you, my friend?"

"Jolly good, as we say in England. Does that mean we are going to stop looking for the treasure?" Milt reacted.

"Just suspend the search. We will have Liu on the case. And, after all, we're going to lose our backer tomorrow," Rid said.

"That's right. Do you suppose we should refund the balance of his $100,000 advance?" Milt joked.

"Not a chance. We earned every penny of that. Maybe we'll even get a reward for his capture," Rid replied.

"Yeah! I'm going over to ask Jeremy about that," Milt grinned as he started to leave. Then he turned and said, "I wonder if this won't get the Prester's Defenders off our backs."

"We need to make certain they learn of the arrest and the fact that we are stopping the search," Rid said.

"Do you think there is anyway we can get one of their curved daggers for our trophy case?" Milt wished.

"I've been wondering when you were going to ask about that. I kept one of the two we got in Maine at Bowdoin College. It's in a the luggage we left at the Intercontinental the day we were kidnapped by Presterman. After the big show tomorrow we'll go get it along with our clothes."

"Jolly good!" Milt chirped again as he crossed the room toward Jeremy Watson.

The conversation over dinner that evening was filled with excitement and anticipation about tomorrow's capture of one of Britain's most wanted criminals.

FIFTY

New York City

The sun was shining brightly as Rid opened his eyes from a surprisingly peaceful night's sleep. After showering and putting on the new suit provided by John Fitzgerald, Rid found Milt and the other safehouse guests already in the dinning room and well into breakfast.

"I was up most of the night reliving our encounters with Dean Floyd back in England at Bodmin Moor," Milt started. "I'm still mad as hell at him and that Franz Schwarz, his henchman."

"How about Schwarz's daughter we met this time? She's more sinister than her dad," Rid added.

"Ouch. Don't remind me of her. I wonder if she'll be there today," Milt squirmed.

"I hope so. We can get her, that Posner guy, and the others involved in our abduction and turn them over to the NYPD," Rid added to the plan.

After breakfast, Rid sent the e-mail to Liu with a very straightforward message of thanks for all her help and good wishes in her new endeavors. He ended the message with, "I doubt that Milt or I will be allowed back in China, but perhaps your work on the palace of Prester John will bring you to Rome to report to your backer at the Vatican. I'll ask Monsignor Corso to keep me informed and to put me down as your dinner companion each time you come. You will always be in our hearts. Affectionately, Rid."

At exactly 9:45, a safehouse car dropped Rid and Milt off at the Lexington Avenue door to the Waldorf Astoria. They entered past a group of plain-clothes people from the various agencies involved. Without any sign recognition they proceeded up the escalator to the lobby floor, went down the corridor to the left past the posh shops and then up the stairs to the foyer of the ballroom.

There were several lines of people at different tables organized by the alphabet to check in the stockholders. At one end was a table marked for press members. They separated themselves by three other reporters who were arriving and waited to have their credentials checked. Milt had slicked back his hair and Rid had on a pair of half glasses as their only disguises. They cleared the check-in without incident. Then they went through one of three metal detectors and were ushered into the ballroom. It was huge and very ornate in its decor. The stage at the far end had a long table draped in green felt across the front with a podium at one end. There were large TV monitors around the room. The focal point, which was commanding the attention of all who entered, was the backdrop of the stage. It was the electrified map of all of EPIC's generating facilities that Rid and Milt had seen back at the company's boardroom the day they were captured. Electricity was leaping across the map from one site to another in all the colors of the rainbow. It was a mesmerizing display.

As the clock struck ten, the room and display went dark. A spotlight shone the door from the third-floor hallway to the left of the stage. First a line of the board members entered and moved to seats in the front row center. Then came the senior officers of the company who ascended the stage to seats at the table. Then a voice offstage said, "Ladies and gentlemen, stockholders of the fastest-growing electric utility in the world, your Chairman, Johnathan Presterman!"

The spotlight followed him across the stage to the podium while the crowd of about 1,800 stood and applauded. He was impeccably dressed, neatly groomed, and exuded confidence and charm.

"Please be seated my fellow shareholders. Welcome to the fifth annual meeting of Energy Producers International Corporation. As you just heard, we are the fastest-growing electric utility in the world. In a few moments I will tell you why we can make that claim. But first to the business of the meeting,"

The head of their nominating committee read the list of candidates for the board while each in turn stood in front. Nominations were quickly closed, tellers were appointed to count the ballots from any who had requested them at check-in. The proxies previously solicited were more than enough to elect the slate, but the tellers retired to get the overall count.

Then Presterman began about a twenty-minute dissertation about the company's growth and financial results, using slides and videos of the facilities around the world. As each site or acquisition was discussed, its light on the map sparkled, remained lit, and began shooting current back and forth to the others that were already lit. It grew by the close of his remarks to the full show that greeted the attendees.

"Now let me close this portion of the meeting by having you meet the people of our great company."

The room went dark, with the exception of the electric grid, and the videos began showing happy workers from each nation, hard at work and talking about how good it was to work for EPIC. During the video, Rid and Milt were able to ease up to their desired positions.

After the video, Presterman returned to the podium, announced that the directors had been overwhelmingly elected. Then he began to take questions from the floor. Microphones had been placed in each aisle about every ten rows, with an usher at each. Anyone wishing to ask a question would go to the closest mike and give their name to the usher who would introduce them to the Chairman. Many of the professional shareholders were known to Presterman and he would welcome them and make some reference to their particular cause. This pleased them greatly. As technical or financial questions were asked, the staff would go through answer sheets on the table and pass them to Presterman. By the time he repeated the question, he had the exact answers in front of him.

After a dozen or more good questions with well-rehearsed answers were done, a small nun went to the microphone. She was introduced as Sister Mary McDonohue from the Sisters of the Poor.

"Welcome Sister Mary. Have you traveled far?" Presterman asked.

"Only from New Jersey, sir. But my question comes from faraway Ireland. I see by your lovely electric map that you have no holdings in Ireland. As you know, there is a great deal of trouble there in the North with great discrimination against the good Catholic workers. So much so a set of principles, the McBride principles, were developed to help the situation. My question is, sir, whether or not you would consider an acquisition there and, if so, would you adopt these principles?"

"We have not considered any acquisitions in Northern Ireland or in the south. Their industry is very closely controlled and difficult to make profitable. My understanding of the McBride principles is that the English government in the North also has a set of antidiscrimination principles which they require companies to follow. While I sympathize with the problems there, I don't see us anytime soon operating in Ireland."

Rid had moved to a mike and given his name as Lynn Merritt. He was introduced.

"Welcome Mr. Merritt. He's from the *Wall Street Journal* staff, ladies and gentlemen, and his analysis reports have been very kind to EPIC."

"Now that the good sister has brought up problems in the U.K., I want to bring up another. I am not Lynn Merritt," he said as he removed his glasses. 'Nor are you Johnathan Presterman. Isn't it true that your real name is Dean Floyd and that you are wanted for treason in England?" Rid raced to get it out before his mike went dead.

Floyd look as if he'd seen a ghost. He started to stammer for security.

At that moment, Milt grabbed the mike near him and he shouted, "It is true. I represent the British government and we are here to arrest this impostor."

Presterman tried to step back, but he tripped on the small table that had held water for him to drink. He stumbled backward and fell against the electric grid. The current coursed through his body as he was electrocuted in front of 1,800 screaming shareholders.

At the first sounds of the shouting inside, the doors were all opened by police. Roy Posner, Frau Schwarz, and the security staff were quickly led away to waiting police vans in the garage below the hotel. Bryan Robert went on stage and asked for calm. He asked the board and other staff to remain while the shareholders were asked to check out at the table they used when they arrived to verify their addresses.

Rid met Milt at the front of the stage. "Wow! How was that for poetic justice, my friend?"

"Very electrifying, my man," Milt replied.

Bryan, Ridley, Milt, Jeremy, and Chief Barnes then met with the board and officers to show confirming evidence about the dual life of Floyd as Presterman.

Bryan told the board, "Once we've interviewed Posner, there may be more arrests of anyone who had knowledge of the truth EPIC, however, is a legal company, and we see no reason for the government to take control. The Justice Department will make a separate investigation sometime soon, and we expect your full cooperation. For now, this board is in charge and you have some senior management openings. We'll leave you to your meeting. You have a company to run."

Once outside, Bryan turned to Milt and Rid and said, "You said you wanted theatrics. Boy did you get them."

"I'll say!" answered Milt. "It was great. And we just saved the Queen a whole lot of money and embarrassment." He turned to Jeremy. "Let's talk some more about that reward."

"I told Milt it was an electrifying end for this case," Rid said.

He then took Milt by the arm and said with a smile, "Let's go across the street, get that dagger, and go home."

EPILOGUE

Rome

It had been just over two years since the death of Dean Floyd, or Johnathan Presterman. The Justice Department of the United States, after their review of EPIC, decided not to take over the company. The new board of directors was doing a good job and the company was sound.

It was time for Dr. Wu Ling and Liu Chow Lim to make their fourth semi-annual trip to Rome, They came every six months to report to Monsignor Corso at the Vatican on their "dig" at the site of Prester John's palace. This time the Curator had invited the head of the Vatican's Foreign Affairs Council and the Pope's Chief of Staff to sit in on the meeting. He also had invited Ridley Taylor and Milt Young, his friends from Janus International, since they had provided the evidence to gain the Vatican's financial support for the excavation. When all were seated, Corso introduced Dr. Ling.

"My English not so good, my Latin less. We have big news. So, have asked Assistant, Dr. Lim to explain."

Liu rose and said, "We have found a portion of Prester John's treasure."

Excitement filled the room. "Go on, please!" the Chief of Staff urged.

Ridley beamed with pride.

Liu continued. "It is not vast. But we have found an old leather trunk that was buried under the palace's main hall floor. We were just finishing the restoration of the mosaic map that covered the floor, when one corner caved in. The trunk was in a hole about four meters by seven meters and five meters deep. We are not yet sure if this is the only hole or chest. We are now looking for more."

"What was in the chest?" Ricardo wanted to skip the details and get to the treasure.

"I have pictures, and something special for your Museum, Monsignor. I was just trying to build the excitement." With that, Liu reached into her bag and extracted an ornate gold cross, inlaid with precious stones. There were emeralds, sapphires, carbuncles, topazes, chrysalides, onyxes, beryls, sardonyxes, and other stones, just like those described in Prester John's letter to Emperor Manuel I of Byzantium.

Everyone rose to gather around this remarkable find. Not just to touch such an important relic, but to feel the truth that a Christian king did exist and was trying to spread Christianity in Asia in the 1100s.

"This will have a place of significant honor in our Museum," Corso said. "May we keep it?"

"Yes," she replied. "Our government has given permission for you to have it."

"Thank you. This is a remarkable piece. The Pope must see it. He will want to conduct a High Mass to consecrate the cross. Scholars and clerics from around the world will come to see this living proof of the legend of Prester John."

"It is a wonderful gift. The Vatican is most grateful," the Foreign Affairs leader said. "We will continue our funding of your excavation."

"Thank you!" Dr. Ling understood those words.

"Let's see the pictures," Milt suggested.

They passed them around. There were two more similar crosses, a number of statues, plates and cups that could have been used in the Sacraments, and a number of loose precious stones.

"What will be done with these?" Corso asked.

"The most exciting thing for us," Liu replied. "The National Museum in Beijing is to dedicate a Prester John room for their display. It will have a full description of Dr. Ling's and my work. We are most honored. It will have a plaque acknowledging the support of the Vatican. They want you all to come for the dedication."

"Including us?" Rid asked, remembering that he and Milt were not welcome in China.

"Yes, including you two. They know you initiated the project."

"Any black suits been around?" was Milt's question.

"Early on, our government deported those remaining in China. Now we hear they are happy we have been restoring the site. We feel they will be pleased with the way we will honor the Prester through the display."

"Then we are coming. I wouldn't miss it for anything," Milt chirped.

Later, over dinner, Rid said to Liu, "I am so happy and proud for you. It has been very special for me to have been in a small way a part of your success."

Liu leaned over and gave Rid a big kiss. "I am very happy with the life you have given me. I will always cherish our friendship. You gave me Prester John."

Prester John, myth or mystery, hoax or history? Perhaps no one can say for sure. This story assumed he lived. But, in the end, you, the reader, must decide.